Hellish
Book Two:
The Chosen

By Scott Dokey

Dedicated to my awesome father who is watching down on me from above. I miss our weekly fishing trips to the little lake down the road.

Out of the night that covers me,
Black as the pit from pole to pole,
I thank whatever gods may be
For my unconquerable soul.

In the fell clutch of circumstance
I have not winced or cried aloud.
Under the bludgeonings of chance
My head is bloody, but not unbowed.

Beyond this place of wrath and tears
Looms but the Horror of the shade.
And yet the menace of the years
Finds and shall be unafraid.

It matters not how strait the gate,
How charged the punishments of the scroll,
I am the master of my fate,
I am the captain of my soul.
—William Ernest Henley

Chapter 1

The Himalayas.

For ages, they have ignited the imagination of countless legends and devotees. The most glorious of them was the Dhankar Monastery. Crowned like a royal fortress on the highest cliff of the Spiti Valley, it watched over the Spiti River that glittered and roared far below. The monastery had concealed its ancient mysteries and miracles, uncorrupted by modern society. This was its greatest power. Its inhabitants tasted a bliss and peace that few could comprehend. Only the fearless and daring braved to scale the harsh and dangerous mountain slope to reach it. But once they did, they were met by a blaze of light and music that overwhelmed them with awe and ecstasy that made them never want to leave.

But a hidden world of mystery and power lay under the earth's surface unknown to the human world. In the dark depths of the underground, a huge cavern shone with a faint light. The walls of the colossal cavern were inscribed with ancient symbols of power, forged by the hands of forgotten masters. They formed a barrier of arcane force that repelled any unwelcome visitors. In the heart of the chamber, a luminous pool shimmered with mysterious light. The

Archangel Michael gazed into its depths with a troubled expression on his face. Flanking him were his fellow archangels: Gabriel on his right and Azrael on his left.

"It's time to reveal everything," he said. "His soul is struggling right now and we are running out of time."

He turned toward Gabriel. "Go quickly. Show him everything. In the meantime, Azrael and I shall prepare the army for battle."

***

He found Michael huddled on a park bench, staring blankly into a small pond before him. Even though the weather outside was balmy, Michael was scrunched up close to himself, his knees pulled up to his chest on the edge of the bench, and shivering visibly. His eyes bore the sadness of a thousand tortured souls in them.

"Michael Davis?" Gabriel asked.

Slowly, Michael turned his head and thought for a moment that he must be dreaming again, caught up in another maddening nightmare that would soon turn into a dark struggle for his sanity.

Gabriel sat down next to him. "Don't be afraid. I'm not here to harm you," he said. "I'm here to help."

"How can you possibly help?" Michael asked. "I don't even know you?"

"But I know you. And I also know that the nightmares are over. They won't bother you again."

Michael was shocked. "How do you know about that?"

"I know everything, Michael, and I've been sent here to help. My name is Gabriel, and I'm one of the Archangels."

"Now I know I'm fucking crazy!" Michael laughed.

Gabriel remained calm, "Look into my eyes and you'll see

that I speak the truth."

Michael turned his head and was instantly spellbound. Perfection radiated in those eyes. A wave of tears engulfed him as he felt the totality of his own imperfections, recalling each moment he had slipped into darkness, too weak to fight his own personal demons.

Gabriel touched his shoulder gently, and he felt a soothing warmth flow through him.

Michael looked up at Gabriel. "Why is this happening to me?"

Gabriel was thoughtful for a minute before he spoke. "It's all quite simple in its reason. It's the never-ending struggle of good versus evil. Only this time, Belial has come up with a plan so diabolical, so ingenious in its manufacture, that he may succeed."

Michael didn't know what to make of the stranger sitting next to him. "Who is this dick, Belial, and why does he keep trying to kill me?"

Gabriel chuckled. "Belial is one of the fallen angels that served Lucifer and was cast out when he was defeated. He was his first in command and feels like he was wrongly expelled from Heaven. Now, he's trying to weasel his way back in."

Michael was stunned as he tried to wrap his head around what he'd just heard. "But what does any of that have to do with me?"

Gabriel looked at him for a moment, measuring Michael's countenance. "Ages ago, we put in place a weapon that we may use against evil if the situation ever called for it. You are that weapon, Michael."

Michael's jaw dropped as the words echoed through his brain, assaulting him as if someone had rung a huge gong only inches from his ears, and his mind once again became a swirling merry-go-round of confusion.

"What the fuck did you just say?" he asked, barely able to get the words out of his mouth.

"Try to calm yourself, Michael," Gabriel said. "I have something I want to show you."

The Archangel vanished for a brief second, only to reappear with a stack of newspapers on his lap. "For you to understand, I must start from the beginning."

He handed the papers to Michael. "Look at these and tell me what you see."

Michael's heart stopped as he saw Harold's face on the cover of the Indianapolis Star. The headline shouted: 'Man takes his own life after family perishes in a gruesome accident'. He devoured the article and realized that it was a mirror of his haunting dream. He tried to push away the images of the man's agony, but they clung to his soul like leeches.

He saw the dead women on the bed as Harold tried to escape the nightmare, their devilish eyes smirking at Michael as they sprang to life in an otherworldly display. He watched sadly as Harold was sentenced to death for crimes he hadn't committed, then heard the slice of the guillotine as it sped downward. Then 'Reverend' was torturing Harold until he had no strength left to fight. Finally, he saw Harold kill himself again.

Michael's face lost all color by the time he finished the article. He turned toward Gabriel, tears falling down his cheeks as he spoke. "I saw him in my dream. It was so clear that I felt like I was there."

"That was a vision you were seeing, Michael. It was not merely a dream, but the future about to happen. The images you saw were very real indeed."

A million questions circled inside of Michael's brain like a horde of vultures waiting to descend upon a dying animal lying on the desert floor. Not one of them issued from his lips, though. Instead, he picked up the next newspaper and started reading.

This one was the Chicago Tribune with the headline: 'Woman leaps to her death after a day of treachery'.

Michael's heart crumbled when he saw Julie's picture radiating happiness on the page. He remembered the sting of failure when she was fired from her job, followed by the blaze of anger and hatred when she witnessed her husband's betrayal and deceit. He recalled the flash when Julie teetered on the narrow ledge, haunted by the shame of her sins. Then he watched her body explode onto the concrete far below. And once again, Belial's image came flying into his brain.

Taking a deep breath before proceeding, Michael picked up the next one. It was the Washington Post this time: 'Wedding day ends in horror after Bride leaves Groom at the altar'.

He had beheld the most splendid day of a man's life turn into a hell of torment. He knew from his own anguish that nothing crushes a man's heart like losing his love. It can rob him of his honor, hurl him into insanity, and annihilate all his sense of self. Here, a man snuffed out his own life because of it. He felt the water choking his lungs again as the monster's jaw clamped onto his leg, while Belial gazed on with cruel eyes.

He placed the paper on top of the other two at his side, leaving Freddy Smith smiling up at him from the L. A. Times on his lap. Beneath his picture was the heading: 'Former NFL star dies of a drug overdose in his downtown apartment'.

Michael had admired Freddy's talent since his college days. Indeed, the whole world had expected Freddy to be a legend for generations to come. Then the unimaginable happened, leaving the sports world in disbelief and Freddie's life shattered. His fall from grace was swift and complete, with no way for him to climb back up. Finally, he had ended his struggle and surrendered to the darkness surrounding him. Then Belial's words rang through Michel's brain, *'You're too late. He's the last one.'*

Slowly, Michael put the paper down on top of the others and looked at Gabriel sadly, wiping the tears from his eyes with the sleeve of his shirt. "These people all went through so much shit until they all believed that suicide was their only way out. And I felt every second."

"You feel that way because you are a compassionate man. In that regard, you are truly a blessed soul. But also know that in these cases Belial had a direct hand in their outcome."

"Yeah, and he also tortured the fuck out of me while he was at it!"

"Your pain is temporary, Michael. I assure you; you will grow to be much more than you are today."

Michael scoffed. "What does that even mean?"

Instead of answering his question, Gabriel continued, "As I stated before, Belial is convinced that Lucifer tricked everyone into following him into battle, knowing that they couldn't win. At first, Belial's anger consumed him and he went on a rampage, searching for evidence to support his claim. Since then, he has grown desperate to return home. We learned of his plan while observing those four individuals as they were being born. Terrible complications developed during each birth, and in a couple of the cases, the mother died. Belial had cursed the souls of these children while still in the womb."

"But why these four?" Michael asked.

"Are you familiar with the book of Revelations?"

Michael felt embarrassed. Here he was, a junkie sitting on a park bench talking to an angel about the Bible, shameful that his ass hadn't touched a church pew as far back as he could remember. "I know a little," he admitted sheepishly, "from when I was younger. Are you talking about the Apocalypse?"

"That's precisely what I mean. However, the book of Revelations points to the fact that the Horsemen are instruments of God. Belial plans to create his own Horsemen that he may use toward his end. As they sow the seeds of death and destruction on the world, he plans to blame the whole thing on Lucifer, and upon defeating Lucifer, he will present himself to our Father as the obedient son he thinks he is. Then the gates will be open to him once more."

Michael was stunned. "Can he win?"

"Possibly. As soon as we realized Belial's plan, we took steps to prepare for his 'manufactured' Apocalypse. In the same way that he doomed those four souls to use for his wicked purpose, we chose four individuals to become weapons against the evil."

Gabriel urged Michael to turn toward the pond, "Look into the pond and I'll show you."

As Michael leaned forward and peered into the water, a small ripple began, starting from the center and working its way outward. Then a series of bubbles rose to the surface from deep below, releasing a foul stench into the air.

A black, inky tentacle suddenly shot out and wrapped around Michael's chest, pinning his arms to his side, and dragged him into the water before Gabriel could react. A final bubble broke the surface of the water before everything went still.

Michael was gone.

Chapter 2

Michael's initial panic nearly killed him when he opened his mouth wide in a terrible scream just as the water closed in on him. It was only by some incredible miracle that his lungs didn't fill with water, sending him to a watery death. His muscles strained under the force of the dark entity that pulled him downward into an abyss that was impossible for the small pond to hold.

Finally, with his ribs at their breaking point, and his lungs on the verge of collapse, he was pulled through a writhing black mass that hung like a curtain separating the fabrics of reality, and thrown into a world that existed both apart and simultaneous to his own.

When the tentacle finally released its hold, Michael found himself on his knees gasping for air on the dirt floor of a cave. His nose was assaulted by an overwhelming smell of decay, while an eerie atmosphere was created by the soft glow of bioluminescent algae on the rock. As his eyes adjusted to the light, he saw an enormous pile of bones stacked near the water's edge, as if something lurking below the surface had discarded them, just like a person throwing their garbage into a dumpster. The light dissipated a short distance out, preventing him from estimating how big the cave was.

The water rippled a brief second before another large bone shot up out of the blackness. The impact dislodged a few on top of the pile and sent them tumbling down to land at Michael's feet. An icy chill ran through him when he saw the human skull staring up at him through its hollow sockets.

As Michael quickly backed away, a figure surfaced. It was Dark and shifty, as if it occupied two planes of existence simultaneously until it stabilized once it had emerged completely. Wearing a finely tailored three-piece suit and tie, the being strode toward him on long legs that ended in a pair of immaculately polished black leather shoes. His hair was perfectly combed, his teeth shiny pearls of white, with the smile of a game-show host spread across his lips. A black cat with fur like midnight rested in his left arm, while he stroked its head with his right hand.

He walked right up to Michael, his smile growing even wider. He bent his head toward the cat, "I bet he has a million questions right now, Abaddon? What do you think?"

Abaddon let out a soft meow in response.

"Who are you?" Michael said through trembling lips as he backed further into the cave.

"There's nowhere for you to escape, Michael," he said. "Consider this the final destination of your failed and miserable life, with me, Nybbas, or 'The Sandman', if you prefer, your host in a final game of 'How fucked up can it get?' And I assure you, if you somehow make it to the final round, you'll wish you'd died a thousand times over."

He leaned close to Michael with a twinkle in his eye. "I heard you like to go on trips? Let's see how you like this one!"

Before Michael could reply, Abaddon opened her mouth wide and a slew of tentacles shot forward and attached themselves to his head, each one with a needle-sharp spine attached to the end that penetrated deep into his skull. The tentacles pulsed and writhed as they pumped his brain with toxins that quickly turned his eyes milky white and rendered him immobile.

"Well, that was easy," Nybbas said. "Now, let's see how long this fucker can survive."

***

Mary turned to Dr. Samuel with fear in her eyes. "What the hell just happened here, Doc?"

Dr. Samuel looked at her apologetically. "He'll be okay. He's just scared."

"No shit!" Mary cried. "So am I. What the fuck is going on?"

"He's letting his fear control him, instead of him controlling his fear."

Mary glared at him. "Yeah, that's fucking easy for you to say. But, how am I supposed to deal with this?"

"Just be there for him when he needs you."

Mary threw her hands in the air and walked toward the door. "That's kind of hard to do when he always shuts me out."

Dr. Samuel watched helplessly as Mary walked out of the room. "Please, be strong for his sake," he said softly as she left.

Shaken to her core, Mary rushed out of the hospital with her phone to her ear. "Come on, Michael, pick up!" she muttered.

After a few minutes, she hung up in frustration. She leaned against the side of the building and sighed, her eyes getting misty.

Mary looked around the parking lot as she walked toward her car, her eyes searching desperately among the crowd of vehicles for any sign of Michael. Just when she was about to give up, a sigh of relief escaped her lips when she saw him leaning against the side of her car with his back to her. "Thank God, you're here! Why wouldn't you pick up when I called?"

Michael didn't answer or turn around. Instead, he just stood there with his shoulders sagged low and his body shuddering as if caught in a sudden chill.

"Please answer me, Michael," Mary pleaded. "I can't help you if you don't talk to me."

Mary walked around the front of the car and gasped when Michael turned to her. His eyes were empty, dark sockets and blood was pouring down his face. He held out his hands, presenting his freshly removed eyeballs to her.

"Maybe the nightmares will go away if I can't see them anymore?" he said through trembling lips, his voice pained and tormented.

Mary's scream echoed through the parking lot, drawing curious stares from nearby onlookers, and causing a handful of pedestrians to come running. The shock of finding herself alone a second later sent her head spinning. Her stomach lurched as she scrambled into the car and slammed the door shut. With trembling fingers, she fumbled the keys into the ignition before finally turning over the engine.

Mary was surprised minutes later when she pulled in front of her apartment building and saw Michael sitting on the bottom step. *How did he get here so fast?* she thought as she turned the car off and paused for a second before getting out. A feeling of dread still engulfed her as she recalled the episode in the parking lot.

Michael got up and walked toward Mary, his face filled

with guilt as he held his arms out to her.

Mary responded with a half-hearted hug.

"I'm sorry," Michael said. "I know I shouldn't have left you like that."

"You're damn right you shouldn't have!" Mary replied. "I'm tired of this shit, Michael. When is it going to stop?"

"It won't happen again. I promise."

Mary looked at him doubtfully.

Michael took her hand and together they walked slowly along the sidewalk that surrounded the apartment complex. Both remained silent for a long time, until Mary finally spoke up. "You can't keep running away like this. I get it. I know you're dealing with some other-worldly shit right now. I've been there. I've seen it too."

"What do you mean?" Michael asked.

Mary cringed inwardly as the image of Michael holding his eyeballs in his hands flashed into her brain for a second. She quickly cast it out. "That doesn't matter. What matters is that we trust each other. I want to help, Michael. But I can't do that if you keep running away."

Michael looked at her sadly. "I'm sorry I've put you through so much. You don't deserve it. You've been more than any man could hope for, and I've treated you like shit. I won't do it again."

"Don't beat yourself up so much. We all go through stuff, and we all treat those who love us like dirt once in a while. It's human nature. It's hard-wired into our DNA."

"Well, I promise not to put you through any more."

They came to a stop, standing at the curb running alongside the main street, which was bustling with traffic at the moment.

"Goodbye, Mary," Michael said somberly before he stepped out onto the street, right in front of a speeding car.

"No!" Mary screamed. But it was too late.

The impact threw Michael's body into the air. A second later, it hit the pavement with a jarring crunch. Tires squealed as Mary rushed into the street where she found Michael lying in a mangled heap.

She leaned over his broken body, his lifeless eyes looking up at her in a curious contented stare that seemed to say, *'now you're free'*. Mary cradled his head in her lap as a wave of anguish spilled from her.

***

Mary jolted up in bed, shaking uncontrollably. After a few seconds, she turned on the bedside lamp and grabbed her phone, checking for any missed calls or texts. Nothing. Finally, she laid her head back down on the pillow, crying softly.

Chapter 3

Brian put the car in park outside the small clinic and turned to his wife with a sly smile on his face. "See, I told you we'd get here in time."

Ruth raised an eyebrow and cocked her head to one side. "Yeah, after driving like a madman for twenty minutes."

"I was not. I was just being a little more aggressive than usual. Besides, everyone knows the cops give you a ten mile an hour cushion."

"Remember those words next time you get pulled over for speeding."

Brian chuckled and turned off the ignition. Neither of them noticed the dark shape that followed them as they get out of the car, moving in and out of the long shadows cast by the late afternoon sun.

Brian held Ruth's hand tight, trying to lend a little encouragement as they walked across the parking lot toward the clinic. Disappointment had been visiting her far too often lately, and he hoped, for her sake, that this trip would turn out different. If not, he was out of answers.

He looked at her and took in the way the soft breeze was gently blowing her hair about as they neared the front door to the establishment. To him, she was perfect, always was and always will be. That she blamed herself for them not being able to start the family of their dreams was ridiculous. But she didn't see it that way. In her mind, something was wrong with her. She was damaged and broken, and nothing he could do or say would convince her otherwise. That's why today was so important.

The clinic was nestled in the center of a small medical complex that housed several private practices. A sign above the entrance read 'New HOPE Clinic'. Stenciled on the door was 'Dr. Phyllis Urbanski, OBGYN'.

"Let's try to stay optimistic," Brian said as he grabbed the handle and opened the door.

"Okay," Ruth replied, not sounding very convincing.

Brian frowned. "Hey, I'm not giving up hope, and I don't want you to, either."

She looked at him and smiled half-heartedly, trying her best to stay positive. "I just hope the doctor has some good news."

"I have a good feeling that today is going to be life changing."

"I wish I shared your enthusiasm," Ruth replied.

As he followed her through the door, Brian felt something cold and chilling flutter past him into the building. He brushed it off as nothing until he felt his cheek tingling. When he reached his hand up, he was surprised to find a cluster of slight bumps forming on his skin, as if he had brushed against something he was allergic to.

He shook off the experience and led Ruth to the counter, where a middle-aged woman with her hair in a bun sat typing on a keyboard.

"May I help you?" the receptionist asked.

Ruth replied, "I have an appointment this afternoon with

Dr. Urbanski. Ruth Summers."

The woman typed on her keyboard once again. "Please, have a seat and we'll call you in shortly."

"Thank you," Brian said.

The receptionist watched them leave the counter with a sly smile on her face and grabbed her cell phone from the desk beside her to make a quick call. "They're here," she said to the entity on the other end.

Ruth kept her eyes low as the two of them entered the waiting room off to the side, averting them from the barrage of child-related objects that adorned the room. Magazines such as *Woman's Day* and *Woman's Health* scattered on the table featuring pregnant women in all their glory; posters and diagrams plastered on the walls depicting the female reproductive organs or the benefits of breast-feeding; these were all stark reminders of a wish unfulfilled.

Ruth sat down quietly on a chair in the corner of the room, with Brian sitting next her. Her face was riddled with anxiety as she fidgeted with her hands nervously.

Across from them, a very pregnant woman sat looking exhausted. Three boys, identical four-year-old triplets wearing the same outfit, sat on her right staring at Ruth quizzically, their heads all bent at a slight and disturbing angle, while Nybbas sat on the woman's left, posing as her husband.

One of boys asked, "Mommy? How come she's not big like you?"

"Hush! That's not a polite thing to ask," the mother scolded. She turned to Ruth, "Sorry, they're still working on their manners."

Ruth replied meekly, "It's okay."

"Maybe she's just getting started having her baby?" the

second boy said. "Is that it? Are you just getting started?" he asked Ruth.

Ruth's eyes misted over.

"That's enough boys!" the mother snapped. "Can't you see the woman's getting upset?"

"Or maybe she's broken and can't have a baby?" the third boy said. "Don't worry, miss. If you can't have a baby, the doctor will fix you."

Nybbas interjected, "Pardon the rudeness of the children. But, he's right. Dr. Urbanski is a miracle worker. With her help, you'll have nothing to worry about."

Nybbas grabbed the woman's hand and squeezed it tightly. "Just look at my fat, little whale of a woman here. She had twelve miscarriages before the doctor came along. Fixed her right up! These handsome boys are the product of her expertise."

The mother smiled at Nybbas and snuggled up against him. "This time it's quintuplets. We're so excited!"

Ruth's eyes grew wide.

Brian's face suddenly grew flush, and a bead of sweat formed on his brow. "I need to go to the bathroom," he said weakly. "I'll be right back."

"Are you okay?" Ruth asked.

"Yeah. It's just a little warm in here."

Brian stood up and had to steady himself, as a wave of dizziness passed through him.

Nybbas got up from his seat and grabbed Brian's arm to steady him. A jolt of electricity passed between them for a brief second.

"You okay there, sport?" Nybbas asked.

Brian nodded before he made his way toward the bathroom at the back of the waiting room.

Once inside, he bent down over the sink and washed his

face with cold water. When he looked up into the mirror, his face rippled and his body spasmed for a second before it settled back into form. His eyes had become dark and brooding, and a game-show host smile spread over his face.

***

The stingers ripped through Michael's skull, unleashing a torrent of burning poison into his brain. He gasped for air, but it was too late. His eyes rolled back in his head, his mind stretched to its limits. He felt a last surge of fear and anguish. Then nothing.

A moment later, he was standing in the corner of a small bathroom, watching the man in front of him unable to fight off Nybbas' possession.

"I see you standing back there in the corner," he heard Nybbas say. "Time for the fun to start!"

Michael's essence was suddenly sucked into Nybbas, and he found himself under the demon's control inside the man's body, much like a puppet under the command of the puppeteer.

"Now, let's see what kind of shit we can stir up?" Nybbas said excitedly.

***

Brian walked back into the waiting area just as the nurse peeked her head into the room. "Ruth?" the young woman said eagerly.

Ruth got up from her seat slowly and joined Brian at the door, her face full of doubt and worry.

"Dr. Urbanski's ready for you," the nurse said. "Follow me."

Nybbas waved happily at the couple with a wide grin on his face. "Good luck!"

The three boys all turned their heads once again at the same creepy angle, each one with a wide, evil, toothy grin plastered on their face that matched Nybbas'.

Brian smiled back at the boys and nodded at Nybbas as he walked toward the door. With a wink, he slid past the nurse, intentionally brushing up against her so that his hand rubbed against her ass, bringing a little giggle from her lips.

The nurse returned the gesture, cupping her hand on Brian's crotch as she walked around them, before proceeding to lead them down a very long hallway with rooms on each side. Some had glass windows showing the room inside, others did not.

Sounds of passion and sex issued from within the hidden chambers, while the rooms with glass windows each showed a mother breastfeeding a newborn child inside.

Soft tears of longing trickled down Ruth's cheeks as she walked along the corridor, tearing the hole in her heart a little wider with each step.

The hallway made a couple of turns until they finally stopped at a door. The nurse pushed the door open. "Have a seat. The doctor will be right in."

As Ruth entered the room, the nurse stopped Brian. "It seems that we need to update your insurance information. If you will follow me, it'll only take a few minutes."

Brian looked at Ruth with a smile. "I'll be back in a minute."

Ruth nodded with an anxious look on her face as Brian followed the nurse down the hall.

As soon as they rounded the corner, out of earshot from Ruth, the nurse slammed Brian against the wall with a fierce hunger. She crushed her lips against his, kissing him with a wild passion that ignited their senses. Their eyes turned pitch black as they clung to each other desperately, consumed by a dark desire.

Brian's form abruptly changed to Michael, bringing a sly smile from the nurse as she ravaged his body. Michael tried to pull back, but the nurse grabbed him tight. "You're not getting away that easy!" she said. "The fun's just starting."

"I don't want to do this!" Michael cried.

Dr. Urbanski sauntered down the hall toward them, her eyes turning black as well as she approached. "Too bad, sport. My game, my rules. Brian, if you will?"

Michael's form changed back to Brian. The nurse immediately planted another firm kiss on his lips before she walked away. "Have fun!" she called back. "Save some for me later."

Brian followed Dr. Urbanski back down the hall toward her office with his hand planted firmly on her ass.

Dr. Urbanski stepped into her office, with Brian close behind her. She turned to Ruth and opened her arms wide for an embrace. Ruth expected a friendly hug, but Dr. Urbanski nearly crushed the wind out of her with the strength of her embrace. "How are you feeling today, Ruth?" she asked as she sat down.

Brian took a seat next to Ruth directly across from Dr. Urbanski. Her eyes locked with his for less than a second, but in that whole time her ice-blue eyes never left his dark pupils. A small, devious smile spread across her lips.

The doctor slowly peeled off her shoe, her gaze fixed on Brian as she crossed one leg over the other. Sliding her foot along his thigh, electric shocks of pleasure tingled under his skin. Ruth remained oblivious to their adulterous movements, sitting complacently next to him.

"To be honest, I'd feel better if you had some good news to

share," Ruth said.

The doctor chuckled. "Actually, I do. Based on the results of your toxicology tests last week, I think there's a good chance one of the fertility drugs we talked about could be effective."

"That's great!"

"But, before we go down that road," the doctor continued, "we need to get to the heart of the issue. I think the real problem is just that you don't put out enough."

Ruth's eyes grew wide and her lips started to tremble. "What do you mean?"

"Come on! Are you that naive? A fine man like this is meant to be worshiped. You should be fucking him every chance you get. There's bound to be a baby in there somewhere."

Tears misted up in Ruth's eyes as she felt the words cut her hard.

The doctor slid off her chair so that she was on her knees in front of Brian. "Would you like me to give you some pointers? Help you spice things up a bit in the bedroom?"

"Why are you doing this?" Ruth cried. "I thought you were my friend?"

"Shut up, you worthless cow! Let me show you what a real woman can do."

***

Michael was powerless to fight the demon as he felt the woman unzip Brian's pants and climb on top of him. Even though it wasn't really him performing the act, every fiber of his being grieved as each thrust felt like a betrayal to Mary's love. Internally, tears streamed down his face.

He heard Nybbas' voice in his head, "You're not trying

very hard, boy! Maybe we need to get you a little more directly involved?"

I don't want to do this, Michael thought. *It feels wrong.*

"Too bad," Nybbas said.

A split-second later, Michael was standing next to the couple as they rode their lust to the frenzy of ecstasy. Although he was in his own body again, he still felt Nybbas' control over him.

"Ooh, another toy to play with!" the doctor exclaimed when she saw him standing there.

Not hesitating for an instant, she forcefully yanked Michael towards her as she continued to undulate wildly on Brian's lap. Her nimble fingers worked swiftly to unlock his clothing restraints from his body. Ruth watched in sheer terror while she caressed and explored Michael's stomach with her long, thin tongue.

Michael glanced over at the woman cowering in the corner, sobbing profusely and begging for her husband to put an end to the madness. He was an outsider who had no idea of her suffering, but he could only imagine the pure horror that she must have been feeling.

"Please stop!" Ruth begged. "Why are you doing this to me?"

Brian and Dr. Urbanski looked over at her and laughed cruelly.

Ruth's pupils dilated in fear as a dark shadow of dread descended upon her. The demons' illusions whispered sinister lies into her psyche, and Michael could feel the oppressive despair radiating from her. Her eyes seemed to sink further and further away, swallowed by an abyss of suffering and terror.

***

"How are you feeling today, Ruth?" Dr. Urbanski asked.

Ruth was jerked back to reality by the doctor's voice, her body trembling with fear. She struggled to compose herself, her head spinning as the horrific images blurred together. In that moment, she felt both helpless and hopeless. As she heard the question, Ruth's mind was pulled in two directions. She both wanted to answer and didn't want to at the same time. Her thoughts tumbled over themselves like a wave crashing against a rocky shore. The images flashing through her mind left her dizzy and disoriented, and she desperately tried to hold on to some sense of what was real. It was as if the terror that had seized her earlier was now doubling down, refusing to let go.

"Sorry, I got lost in my thoughts for a second," she finally said. "To answer your question, I'd feel a lot better if you had some good news to share."

"Actually, I do," the doctor replied. "Based on the results of your toxicology tests last week, I think there's a good chance one of the fertility drugs we talked about could be effective."

A guarded glimmer of hope, like a single drop of dew resting on a blade of grass, popped into Ruth's eyes.

"While nothing's certain," she continued, "it at least gives you guys a chance."

Brian reached out and grasped Ruth's hand, his thumb caressing her palm, looking into her eyes. "Right now, that's all we're looking for," he said.

Ruth responded by giving his hand a tender squeeze in return.

Progress, Brian thought. And when the hint of a smile threatened to cover her face for the first time in a long while, he felt like everything was going to be okay.

"So, what's the next step?" Ruth asked.

Dr. Urbanski replied, "I'm giving you a prescription for Clomid, which is the most common fertility drug on the market. Then the rest is up to you."

She took a small pad from the pocket of her lab coat and scribbled on it for a second before tearing the sheet off and handing it to Ruth. "Just be aware that there may be some side effects—hot flashes, headaches, mood swings—things like that."

Ruth looked at the small slip of paper in her hands as if she were holding a winning lottery ticket. Her eyes misted over as a smile crossed her lips, because in her mind, that's exactly what it was.

Chapter 4

Michael followed the couple out of the doctor's office, his heart hurting for Ruth's anguish. She was an innocent person, yearning for something special in her life, completely unaware that she was caught in a hellish nightmare.

"Don't feel bad for her," Nybbas said. "She'll get what's coming to her. I promise."

"Why are you doing this?" Michael asked.

"First, it's fun as hell to fuck up a person's life and watch it all go to shit. And second, you're my ticket to freedom, boy, so don't have any thoughts about being a hero."

"You're working with Belial?"

Nybbas replied, "Ding, ding, ding! We have a winner. I guess you're not as dumb as you look."

Suddenly, the doctor's words whispered in Michael's head, *'He fears you. And well, he should.'* The beginning of a plan began formulating in his brain. The trick was hiding it from the demon.

Suddenly, the world around Michael shifted, and he found himself skulking in a darkened corner of a drugstore. His eyes widened as he spied a huge, bald man with a bulging gut and beady eyes who had just finished accepting the prescription from the couple. They were oblivious to the mad scientist lab lurking behind him. Vials and flasks perched above hissing burners bubbled and frothed with mysterious concoctions while a partition nearby intoned 'Quality Control' above an area filled with a dozen chairs arranged in three neat rows. The chairs were occupied by individuals in various states of altered consciousness; some snorted their fix of powdery substances, others plunged needles into their veins, while still others thrashed about in the throes of whatever drugs they had ingested.

The pharmacist looked at the prescription and grinned. "Have a seat out front and I'll have it ready shortly."

Brian and Ruth walked away from the counter toward a small seating area in the corner of the store, while the pharmacist shuffled toward the back.

The pharmacist looked at Nybbas with a deceitful look in his eyes. "I have just the thing to spice this up a bit."

Nybbas chuckled. "I bet you do, you dirty old man!"

The man hastened towards the back, with barely contained excitement, unaware of the development unfolding in the front row. Suddenly, one of the test subjects started to convulse violently, foam spewing from her lips in spurts. Scarlet tears ran down her face as her eyes bled profusely while her body shuddered and writhed until it suddenly went limp. In a matter of seconds, her body deflated, stillness consuming her until she lay motionless on the floor.

"Well, that sucks!" Nybbas said. He turned to Michael, "Looks like you're up next! With the job market as tight as it is right now, it's a good thing you're here. Plus, you have the experience to boot. Now, get in there and show me what you got!"

Nybbas slapped Michael on the shoulder. "Have a seat. I insist!"

Michael found himself unable to stop himself as he sat down in the chair just moments after a worker in a janitorial uniform finished whipping mucus and excrement from the seat.

Off to the side, the pharmacist was standing with his back to them, moaning as he added his 'special sauce' into the couple's prescription. The pharmacist winked at Michael as he walked back to the counter and handed the semen covered bag to Ruth.

After the couple exited the drugstore, the man walked over to Michael holding a clipboard in his hand. "Since this is your first day, let's go over some rules first. Then we'll throw you into the fire."

Michael looked at him fearfully.

The pharmacist chuckled. "Don't worry. We're not gonna do anything to you that you haven't done to yourself already. You do have a little bit of a track-record, after all. In fact, you've become kind of a legend around here. Many of those behind you grew up wanting to be just like you."

He looked down at his clipboard again. "Ah, who am I kidding? There aren't any rules. Have fun!"

The pharmacist joined Nybbas in front of the counter.

"How long do you think?" Nybbas asked.

The pharmacist replied, "I give him ten minutes at most."

"Wow, you're much more optimistic than I am. I was thinking half that."

They both watched eagerly as a large black spider-like creature, its body the size of a baseball, with a scorpion tail arching over its head, suddenly scurried up Michael's leg and across his chest. Its fangs clicked anxiously as it perched on top of his shoulder, inches away from his ear. Then it lunged forward and clamped onto his neck as its stinger shot forward, sinking deep into his flesh.

Nybbas walked over and pulled Michael's eyelid up to examine his pupils, which had a far-away look in them. "We'll let that marinate for a while," he said.

Michael suddenly found himself standing in front of his own body, watching in horror as the spider-thing kept pumping venom into his body. His skin was turning deep shades of purple in places, with black veins extending from his neck and disappearing down his chest beneath his shirt.

"You truly are a natural, I'll give you that," Nybbas continued as he bent close to inspect Michael's deteriorating body. "Now, this next round is going to be a show-stopper. And you, Michael, as pathetic as you are, get to decide how it's going to play out. But I'm warning you ahead of time, choose wisely. Every action will have consequences."

Michael watched helplessly as his body in the chair twitched and spasmed sporadically under the relentless attack of the venom pumping through his veins.

***

Ruth sat nervously on the edge of the bed, looking at the box of pills in her hand. Inside was the glimmer of hope that she had asked for—a saving grace—yet something nagged at her. She searched her heart and realized that she was scared. Not that the pills wouldn't work, but that they would. For the first time, she questioned whether she was ready to be a mother.

Brian sat down next to her. "What's wrong?"

Ruth just shrugged her shoulders.

"Are you okay?"

"Yeah, I'm fine. It's just that, for the first time since we talked about having a family, I wonder if I'm ready? I don't know what kind of mother I'm going to be?"

Brian wrapped his arm around her and held her tight. "You have nothing to worry about, dear. You're going to be the best mother in the world. I just know it."

She looked into his eyes and all of her worry instantly faded. "I guess I'm just being silly."

"Yes, you are."

She gave him a soft kiss before she opened the box and pried one of the white pills from the foil pack into her palm.

***

Nybbas put his arm around Michael's shoulder as they watched the couple discuss their future. "Here's the first question of this round, Michael. Think long and hard before you answer. Do you think Ruth should take the pill that might give her the family she yearns for, or should she flush the pill, and with it her dreams for the future, down the toilet?"

I can't do this! Michael thought. *It's not right! How can I decide on someone else's future?* Instead of answering, he stood there speechless, as if remaining silent would make the whole situation go away.

"You're not getting off that easy, sport," Nybbas said. "I'm giving you to the count of three, then they'll both be subjected to a series of hideous tortures before I ultimately decide for you. Therefore, by not making a choice, you are, in fact, actually making a choice."

Nybbas started counting. "One."

Michael's mind raced. He didn't know which way to go? Somehow, he knew that no matter what he picked, it was going to end in disaster for the couple.

"Two," Nybbas continued.

In a panic, Michael quickly said, "Yes! She takes it!"

Nybbas smiled. "Good choice!"

Michael's heart raced in fear as the pill morphed into a squirming insect that she grasped tightly between her fingers. She opened her mouth wide and threw it inside, gulping down the sickly sweet liquid from the glass Brian had handed her. But to Michael's horror, he realized it was not water but an inky sludge that hissed and bubbled as it slid down her throat.

"This is going to be so much fun!" Nybbas said eagerly.

Chapter 5

"Time for you to get back in there," Nybbas said as he slapped Michael on the back once more, like he was on the sidelines being thrown into the game after an injury to the starting quarterback.

Nybbas continued, "I think we'll try a little role reversal this time just for fun."

Michael suddenly found himself looking at Brian through eyes filled with savage lust. He was inside Ruth's body! *No! I don't want to do this again!*

"Too bad, so sad," Nybbas said. "Of course, you can always just surrender and give up like you've done your whole pathetic life."

His words hit Michael like a punch to the gut. They were true. He had always run away from his problems, hoping that they'd disappear when he did. His cowardice shamed him, nevertheless, he couldn't help it. But he knew that if he wanted to survive this time he'd have to fight for his life, even though all his instincts screamed at him to just hide away and hope for the best.

Before he could react, however, he found himself pouncing on Brian, ripping at his clothes feverishly as they fell onto the bed. She climbed on top of him, peeling her clothes off while ravaging his body with her teeth and claws. A sharp cry flew from Brian's lips the first time her teeth sank into his flesh, but then his eyes grew dark and sinister and he embraced the pain. Together, they ripped at each other's bodies until the flow of blood turned the white sheets red. "I want you to fuck me harder than you've ever fucked me before," her desperate voice said.

Michael whimpered when he felt Brian enter her body, making him feel used and violated. As their passion ramped up, his feeling of hopelessness grew. His thoughts of fighting only moments before became pure folly in his brain. How could he possibly fight something so evil?

Ruth rolled off of Brian onto the blood-soaked sheets and lay there spread-eagle, her face twisted with mock guilt. "I've been a bad girl, Brian," she said. "I think I need to be punished."

A devious smile grew on Brian's lips as he straddled her, grabbing a length of rope from the edge of the bed that Michael was sure wasn't there a second ago, and bound Ruth hand and foot tightly to the bed. Michael suddenly had a flashback of the demonic dominatrix in Hell's torture chamber and felt a surge of panic writhing through him.

With each thrust, Michael could feel the wriggling worm inside Ruth's body grow as it fed off of their sexual energy. Before long, it had grown large enough to press against her lungs, making it difficult to breathe.

He heard the sound of a whisper in his mind, compelling him to calm down. He couldn't tell if it was Mary's voice, or Gabriel's, or just his imagination trying to be brave in a hopeless situation, but he clung to it like a life preserver as it buoyed him up from the despair that had threatened to drag him under only moments ago. The strength wasn't enough to keep him from panicking, but it was enough for him to take control from his fear and do what needed to be done.

As their passion soared toward a crescendo, the worm—now the size of a basketball—wriggled and squirmed just below the surface of her skin, giving off an orange glow that illuminated the cramped organs underneath. A pair of thin antennae emerged from her belly button and reached forward to wrap around Brian's body, pulling him further into her. But, just before Brian exploded inside of Ruth, Michael pushed with all of his might and forced himself out of her body.

Nybbas looked at Michael, who was standing next to the bed, with an irritated look on his face. "Consider yourself lucky, boy. I assure you it won't happen again."

***

Six weeks later, Brian stood in the hallway, his eyes wide with worry as he listened to the gagging noises coming from the bathroom. He clenched and unclenched his hands nervously while he waited for the sound of a toilet flushing to quiet before tentatively asking, "Ruth, are you alright?".

Ruth was silent for a moment, before she replied, "Yeah. I'm okay."

She just barely got those words out of her mouth before she started vomiting again. "Maybe I'm not so good after all," she said weakly after the episode was finished. "Just give me a few minutes."

"Okay. I'll be in the next room. Please, call me if you need anything."

"I will."

"I love you," Brian said to bring her spirits up.

"I love you, too."

Brain reluctantly dragged his feet away from the bathroom, desperately wishing he could stay and help Ruth through her torment, but knowing that he had no actual power to change her situation. He wanted to do something; anything, to take some of her pain away, but ultimately there was nothing left for him to do but silently walk away.

***

Ruth's shoulders dropped and she let out a deep, exhausted sigh. With her body slumped against the bathroom wall, she stretched her arm across the tiled floor to grab hold of the toilet handle. She gasped when she saw the floating mass of glistening black mucus, resembling tar more than excrement. "Well, that's disgusting!"

She flushed the toilet and then pulled herself up to the sink. After running a washcloth under the faucet, she wiped her mouth off and plopped it into the sink. She gripped the edge of the sink while she steadied herself. "Holy shit!" she muttered as she sought to recover from the attack.

Her reflection staring back at her in the mirror was startling. Her bloodshot eyes were rimmed with dark circles, and her face was flushed a deep red. A bead of sweat trickled down her temple as she looked at herself and whispered, "God, I look like Hell."

Ruth shuddered as she ran the washcloth under the faucet once again, her heart pounding in her chest. Taking a deep breath, she lifted it to her face and froze, horrified by what she now saw in the mirror. It was still her reflection, but it seemed out of control, moving independently, lagging behind her body's movements like an eerie ghost. The longer she stared the more discordant they became, until finally it twisted to the side with an unnatural gesture, lifting its shirt and exposing a swollen pregnant belly beneath. Then Ruth's eyes widened in horror as the mass inside shifted and undulated, until a demonic face pushed against the skin from within, stretching it so thin that she could almost see through it. She screamed and stumbled back, landing on the toilet seat. When she looked back up, the image had vanished.

Brian rushed into the room a moment later. "Are you okay? What's going on?"

Shaking visibly, Ruth took a moment to gather herself. "I'm okay. I just thought I saw something."

"Like what?"

Ruth pushed her terror down, discounting the gruesome visage as a product of her current state. She shook her head. "It was nothing. I'm just not feeling well. I think I'm running a fever."

Brian held Ruth tight as he led her from the bathroom. Neither of them noticed Ruth's reflection smiling at them with a wide, demonic grin spread across her face as they left.

After gingerly leading her down the hall and into the bedroom, Brian cradled Ruth in his arms as he helped her into bed. As he did, her shirt lifted a little and he noticed a large red mark forming on her side. He pulled her shirt up and was surprised to see that the mark ran all the way up her side from her hip to her arm-pit.

"How did you get that? Brian asked in shock.

Ruth was confused for a second and looked down. When she saw the mark, she flashed back immediately to the image of her reflection in the mirror, and the demonic face trying to push through her skin.

She pushed the image out of her mind quickly, trying to hide her fear from Brian. "I don't know? Might be from lying on the floor in the bathroom?"

Brian looked at her skeptically, suspecting that she was

hiding something. "Just keep an eye on it. We might need to talk to Dr. Urbanski if it gets worse."

Ruth nodded quietly.

He bent down and kissed her on the forehead. "Try to get some rest. You'll feel better in a bit."

"I hope so," she replied softly, tears clouding her eyes as Brian left the room.

Chapter 6

Mary shot up in bed and frantically grabbed her phone, desperately searching for any sign of life from Michael. Nothing.

After a few moments of quiet frustration, she slowly dragged herself out of bed and ambled to the window, staring absentmindedly at the courtyard below. She jumped when her phone jingled with an incoming call, but quickly felt her spirit dampen when she saw that it was only a telemarketer. Anger surged through her as she muttered under her breath, "No! I am not doing this," and stormed out of the room. Her thoughts raced as she grappled with conflicting emotions. On the one hand, she wanted desperately to hear from him. On the other, if he didn't care enough to let her know where he was, why should she even bother?

Just as Mary stepped into the cramped living room of her tiny apartment, a muffled thumping sounded from her door. A crease formed on her forehead before she cautiously bent down and peered through the peep-hole. She slowly turned the lock and pulled open the door.

Nybbas was standing in the hall with a friendly smile on

his face.

"Can I help you?" Mary said.

"Are you Mary?" Nybbas replied.

"Depends on who wants to know?"

"I'm a friend of Michael's. My name is Nick."

Mary eyed Nybbas suspiciously. "He's never mentioned a Nick before."

Nybbas chuckled. "That's not surprising. We met under less-than ideal circumstances, if you know what I mean?"

"Not really."

"That doesn't matter right now. What's important is that Michael's okay. He's just working through some stuff."

A feeling of dread flashed through Mary's eyes. "Where is he? Does he need my help?"

Nybbas replied, "Actually, he told me to tell you that he doesn't want your help. He said that you've helped enough already."

Mary's lip started to quiver.

"I'm sure he'll call soon," he continued. "In fact, he'll likely be a changed man when you see him again.

As Mary stood there in silence, Nybbas nodded his head toward her. "It was good to meet you, Mary. Who knows, maybe we'll run into each other again sometime?"

Nybbas turned and walked down the hall.

Mary peeked her head into the hallway a second later, but Nybbas was gone. A shiver ran through her as she closed the door. "Well, that wasn't creepy at all," She mumbled.

***

Ruth rolled over and winced at the ache that had settled in her body overnight. It took her a few moments to adjust to the light streaming through her bedroom window, and then she propped herself up with one arm so that she could look at the red mark on her side. She felt a wave of relief when she saw that it was beginning to fade, but still couldn't shake the uncomfortable feeling it left behind. Gently, she traced its outline with her finger.

Her stomach gave a loud rumble, and before she could even attempt to stand up, Ruth was overcome by a dizzying sensation that sent her tumbling back onto the bed. Once the dizziness faded, she called out, "Brian?"

When Brian didn't answer after a few seconds, she called out even louder. "Brian?"

Still nothing. Finally, she cried out at the top of her lungs, "Brian?!"

Brian frantically rushed into the room a moment later, his face contorted in a blind panic. "What's the matter? Are you okay?"

Ruth replied matter-of-factly, "I'm hungry."

Brian's jaw dropped as he looked at her in shock. "Say what?"

"I said, I'm hungry. Starving, actually."

"You screamed like that because you were hungry?"

"Well, you didn't come the first two times I called you."

"I was in the living room watching TV."

"I figured as much, hence the screaming."

"Why didn't you come out and get me?"

"I tried to get up and got dizzy," Ruth replied, right before her stomach growled again, this time with a vengeance.

Brian looked at her apologetically. "Okay, Your Highness, what can I get for you?"

Ruth's eyes scrunched together as she thought for a second. "How about pickles and ice cream?"

"Isn't that a little cliché?"

Ruth chuckled. "Just playing. Actually, a pizza sounds

really good. Lots of cheese and pepperoni...and add olives to it. And while we're waiting for the pizza to be delivered, I think there's a tub of mint chip ice cream in the freezer."

Brian cocked an eyebrow. "Anything else?"

"Maybe a glass of milk too?"

Brian made a mock bow before he turned and left the room.

**

When the doorbell rang, Brian rushed to the door, opening it to reveal Nybbas standing there holding a large pizza in his hands, disguised as a pizza delivery man. "Thank God, you're just in time!" he said with relief gleaming in his eyes. "Another few minutes and I'm pretty sure my wife would start gnawing on her own fingers!"

Nybbas chuckled. "Let me guess: pregnant?"

Brian answered, "Yep!"

"Morning sickness? Weird cravings? Mood swings?"

"You sound like you're talking from experience."

"Let's just say I've been around for a while. How far along is she?"

"Six weeks. I'm just hoping the morning sickness goes away. She doesn't do well with getting sick."

Ruth's voice suddenly bellowed from the bedroom. "Brian? Is that the delivery guy?"

"Speaking of the devil. I better get this in there, fast."

"I think that would be wise."

Brian reached into his pocket for his wallet but Nybbas stopped him.

"Don't worry," Nybbas said. "I got you covered. Consider it my contribution to your family's future."

"Thanks, man!"

"No problem. Just promise me that you'll embrace the chaos this pregnancy going to bring?"

Brian gave a confused nod toward Nybbas before he closed the door.

When Brian entered the room, Ruth's eyes grew wide. "Thank God! I'm famished!"

He eyed the empty tub of ice cream on the nightstand, its residue dripping down the side and pooling around the equally empty glass of milk next to it, and wondered how in the world she could still be this hungry?

She snatched the pizza box from Brian's hands and immediately began stuffing her face.

Brian watched her in shock for a moment. "Is there anything else you need? A napkin, perhaps?"

"Another glass of milk," Ruth replied with her mouth full, sending little streams of grease running down her chin.

Brian stood frozen in the doorway, his stomach churning at the sight of Ruth's feral feast. She consumed her food with a ferociousness he'd never seen, her hands and face covered in a repulsive mixture of grease, sauce, and saliva that had been smeared all over her shirt and sleeves. He watched in disgust as she wolfed down bite after bite, unable to look away from the gruesome scene unfolding before him.

***

Michael followed Brian down the hallway, with Nybbas walking beside him.

"So, Michael, how are you enjoying our little excursion here so far?" Nybbas asked.

Michael didn't answer.

"While I'm certain it probably doesn't rank up there with some of your previous trips, I'm quite impressed with my sense of creativity so far."

Michael remained silent.

"I should also mention that I paid your woman a visit recently. She's a cute little thing. I'd certainly like to get a piece of that action!"

Michael turned angrily toward Nybbas. "Don't you dare touch her, or I swear—"

Michael's mouth suddenly disappeared.

"You were saying? Actually, I was just shitting you. She's a little beneath my standards."

As they arrived at the bedroom door, Michael's mouth reverted back to normal. He looked inside the room and was stunned to see Ruth sitting on the bed with her back propped up against the wall. She had a slice of pizza in each hand and switched back and forth from each one, eating feverishly. A large squid-like beak jutted from her stomach, chomping hungrily, while four large tentacles shoveled pizza slices into the monstrous mouth.

Michael exclaimed, "What the Hell?"

"Now you're catching on!" Nybbas said.

Michael watched in terror as Brian entered the room, unaware of the monstrosity on the bed, and gave Ruth a glass of milk. She gulped the liquid down greedily, spilling it down the front of her chin onto her shirt. A loud belch flew from her mouth, echoed by a loud growl from the beast within her.

Chapter 7

Ruth jolted awake, her face contorted in agony. She sucked in a deep breath, trying to find relief from the sharp pain slicing through her. Her stomach rose and fell with each heaving intake of air as she placed her trembling hands onto her swollen abdomen. A low whimper escaped her lips before another piercing scream echoed off the walls.

"Brian? I think it's time!" she called out as she pushed herself out of bed once the pain subsided.

When there was no answer, Ruth waddled out of the bedroom, walking slowly down the hallway, bracing herself against the wall with one hand while supporting her stomach with the other.

"Brian? Did you hear me?" she called out again with a hint of desperation creeping into her voice.

The house remained eerily silent.

She came to the end of the hallway and peered into the living room, only to find it empty. "Brian?"

Another contraction wracked through her and she steadied herself against the wall for a minute as it passed.

Ruth's heart pounded as she made her way to the kitchen, fear gripping her like a vise. When she found the room empty, an icy chill spread through her. "Brian? Where are you?" her trembling voice echoed throughout the house.

A faint knock from the bedroom sent her scrambling desperately into the hall. With a feeling of dread roiling through her, she peered into the room and was met with nothing but silence. Tears streaming down her face, Ruth cried out between sobs, "Brian! Please answer me! We need to get to the hospital right away! Where are you?!"

She shuffled to the adjoining bathroom and looked at herself in the mirror. Her face was gaunt and pale; her eyes bloodshot, with dark circles around them. She looked like Death warmed over.

Another contraction took hold, this time stronger than before. Ruth slunk to the floor crying desperately. "Please, Brian...I need help!"

A pool of blood began to spread out from between her legs, covering the entire bathroom floor in a matter of seconds. A violent scream erupted from her as she felt both her and her baby's life drifting away.

***

As Ruth opened her eyes, she was hit with a wave of dizziness and felt an intense sensation of déjà vu course through her body. Her stomach throbbed, and she gasped in pain as she clutched her abdomen tightly. Tears welled up in her eyes and she lay still for a few minutes before her breath evened out and the pain ebbed away. With effort, Ruth pushed away the covers and sat up in bed, feeling a chill from the cool air in the room.

Brian was sitting at the table, absorbed in his daily routine of coffee, toast, and the morning newspaper. And when he was reading the sports section, he rarely noticed much of anything else, which is why he didn't notice Ruth when she entered the kitchen.

"Brian, it's time," Ruth stated through clenched teeth.

"What do you mean it's time?" Brian asked dully, "Time for what?"

"Well, if you'd put that newspaper down for a second, I think you'd be able to figure it out."

Brian dropped the paper with a slight look of irritation on his face. He immediately saw that a small puddle of water had gathered on the floor at her feet and the front of her pants was wet, but for a second, he sat there confused, until his brain caught up with his eyes and he understood what was going on. Ruth's water had broken. They were going to have a baby. Now!

Like every typical father-to-be, Brian ran about frantically, trying to get everything ready. "Are you packed yet? Is everything ready? Do we need to call an ambulance?" he asked quickly, as he grabbed hold of her hand a little too hard.

"Yes, yes, and no. The suitcase is by the front door. Everything is taken care of. And no, we don't need to call an ambulance."

Brian's face turned red. "I'm sorry...just a little anxious, I guess. Have you timed your contractions yet?"

"About four minutes apart."

"What about the doctor?"

"Already called her a minute ago."

"What about—"

"Already taken care of."

"But you don't even know what I was going to say."

Ruth looked at her husband in amusement. "Doesn't matter. Whatever it was, I already took care of it."

Brian smiled. "Okay, I get the hint. I'll pull the car into the driveway and we'll be off."

He stopped at the doorway and looked back at his very pregnant wife, his face beaming. "I love you," he said tenderly.

"I love you too, dear. Now let's go, unless you want to deliver this baby yourself right here on the living room floor."

She didn't have to say that twice! A second later, Brian was flying out the door to his car. He backed up quickly, getting as close to the house as possible without crashing through the garage door.

As Ruth settled into the seat, she looked up to see a large, black cloud pass in front of the sun that cast them into momentary darkness. The sense of dread that had attacked her earlier suddenly returned. She shook the feeling from her as Brian pulled out of the driveway, and a minute later, they were speeding toward the hospital.

***

Brian aggressively drove through town, with Ruth crying out through clenched teeth and holding on for dear life, both of them completely unaware of the passengers in the back seat.

"As you can see," Nybbas said, "I've skipped forward a bit to avoid the unnecessary whining and sniveling from the woman going through her hormonal roller-coaster. That first trimester was almost more than I could bear. I certainly didn't want to go through that again!"

Michael sat next to Nybbas cowering in fear.

The sky overhead grew dark as storm clouds quickly moved in. Nybbas peered out of the window. As he did, the largest cloud changed shape and a demon's face grinned back at him.

"Beschaud!" Nybbas said excitedly. "Right on cue!"

The storm demon let out a mighty roar that shook the ground, then the clouds opened up and a torrent of rain poured down.

***

Brian turned the windshield wipers on as fast as they could go, but visibility had been reduced terribly. Craning his neck forward, as close to the windshield as he could get, he drove forward in the downpour.

A car loomed suddenly in front of them and he hit the brakes to avoid a collision. Ruth let out a stifled scream as she braced herself for the impact, but the car came to a screeching-halt inches from the other vehicle.

"Slow down, Brian!" Ruth begged.

"I'm going as slow as I can!" Brian replied. "I can't see a damn thing in this rain!"

"Maybe we should just pull over and wait until it passes?" Ruth suggested.

"But, what about the baby? We don't know how long this storm is going to last? It could keep going like this for hours!"

As if to answer him, another contraction surged through Ruth, causing her to cry out. She looked at Brian worriedly. "Just be careful."

Brian nodded as he pushed lightly down on the accelerator and proceeded slowly forward.

***

A huge pot-hole nearly brought the trip to a halt a few blocks later as the car slammed down hard, causing Michael to hit his head on the ceiling of the car.

"Watch your head there," Nybbas said with a grin. "We've still got a ways to go. Don't want you missing out on the fun."

Michael grumbled at Nybbas.

"Now, pay attention here," Nybbas said. "This next one's gonna be a doozie."

Michael gasped in horror when he saw a car spinning out-of-control heading straight for them from the opposite direction. As the twirling vehicle got closer, he closed his eyes and braced for impact.

The scene suddenly jumped forward, and they were standing in the hospital near the reception desk, where Brian was talking to the receptionist as Ruth struggled to mask her agony next to him. Michael looked around confused, completely disoriented.

"You okay there, sport?" Nybbas asked. "You look a little out of sorts."

Michael opened his mouth to say something and then quickly closed it again.

Nybbas chuckled.

Brian finished checking Ruth in at the desk as a nurse brought a wheelchair over and helped her sit down.

"I'll think you'll appreciate this next little twist," Nybbas said.

Michael was surprised to see Dr. Urbanski come out to meet the couple a minute later. After a small exchange, she grabbed the handles and wheeled Ruth toward the elevator, with Brian walking alongside.

"I knew you'd be surprised," Nybbas said. "Just wait until the fun really starts!"

Fear swept through Michael as he dared to even guess what kind of horror the demon had schemed up.

***

As they rode the elevator up to the third floor, a look of concern crossed Dr. Urbanski's face when she saw the sweat pouring out of Ruth and the pale complexion of her skin.

"How are you feeling, Ruth?" she asked.

"I'm okay," Ruth replied, "just ready to get this kid out of me!"

Dr. Urbanski chuckled. "It'll be over soon enough. I promise."

The elevator finally stopped, and the doctor wheeled Ruth toward the birthing suites at the end of the hall. Brian kept stride with them on her left side, squeezing Ruth's hand tightly to comfort her.

Dr. Urbanski stopped for a moment at the nurse's station to give instructions to the staff, while two nurses followed them into the suite. They helped lift Ruth out of the wheelchair and eased her onto the hospital bed in the center of the room before the doctor opened a panel at the end of the bed and withdrew the metal stirrups.

With Ruth's feet propped up, she did a preliminary exam. "You're dilated about three centimeters, so you have a little while to go yet. However, we have another problem. The baby is in breach right now, so we need to keep the possibility open that we'll have to perform a C-section. It's too early to worry, though. There's a very good chance that he'll turn soon and everything will be fine."

"It's her," Ruth interjected. "Her name is Isabelle."

Dr. Urbanski chuckled. "Sorry, just a little Freudian slip. I was the one who did the ultrasound. Isabelle is a beautiful name."

During this exchange, one of the nurses took Ruth's blood

pressure, while the second took her temperature. The doctor frowned when she saw that both readings were a little higher than she would've liked.

She turned to Ruth, "Tell me honestly, how are you feeling right now?"

"Actually, at the moment, I feel exhausted. My lips are a little numb. I'm chilled and sweating at the same time, and I think I have a fever. Beyond that, I feel fine."

"It looks like you're in the early stages of toxemia. It's pretty common, so don't panic. The first thing we'll do is start an IV to help get your blood pressure down. Then we'll hook up a monitor, which will take a reading every ten minutes."

Ruth didn't like the idea of a blood-pressure cuff squeezing her arm like a python every few minutes, but she didn't really have a choice and nodded quietly.

"And if you're okay with it, I'd like to administer an epidural to help with the pain."

"Do we have to? I've heard horror stories about those things."

"I think it's probably the best course of action right now. I promise, the procedure will go smoothly."

Ruth looked at her for a second and then gave in. "Okay, you win."

The doctor grabbed Ruth's hand and squeezed tightly, looking into her eyes with the tender love of a genuine friend. "Don't worry, Hon," she said softly, "everything's going to be fine."

Before Ruth could say anything, the doctor was on her way out the door with a look of concern on her face.

Brian's voice betrayed his fear as he tried his best to comfort Ruth. "You heard the doctor. Everything's going to be fine, dear. It's all just precautionary stuff to make sure nothing crazy happens. She even said this is a pretty common condition for pregnant mothers."

Ruth sighed, "I guess you're right." She didn't have the strength anymore to be her usual stubborn self. She closed her eyes and tried to convince herself that everything would be alright, but as she lay uncomfortably in bed, she couldn't help but feel that something bad was waiting for her in the shadows. The dread that had covered her earlier came back with a vengeance, and she knew this time it wouldn't leave.

The IV drip started and Ruth felt a slight pressure building up in her veins. She turned her head towards the window, trying to distract herself from the discomfort. But the feeling of something lurking in the dark corners of her mind was growing stronger with each passing moment.

"We'll be back in a couple of minutes to check on you," one of the nurses said. "If you need anything, press the button on the side of the bed."

Ruth responded with a weak nod, while Brian responded, "Thank you."

"Why don't you close your eyes and try to get a little rest," Brian said after the nurses left the room.

"Okay," Ruth replied hoarsely.

The thickness in her voice concerned Brian as he watched her close her eyes and drift into a restless sleep.

***

Ruth heard a scratching noise, like sharp claws on the tile floor, that jolted her wake. She turned her head toward the sound and immediately her heart started racing when she saw a shadowy figure in the corner of the room. She blinked, and it was gone. As was Brian. Terror instantly grabbed hold of her.

Ruth felt a cold shiver run down her spine. She tried to sit up in bed, but her body felt numb and heavy. She tried to scream, but no sound came out of her mouth.

Suddenly, the figure appeared again. This time, it was standing right next to her bed, staring down at her. Its eyes were dark and empty, and its face was twisted into a malicious grin.

Ruth tried to move, her hand searching for the panic button, but her body wouldn't budge. She was completely paralyzed.

Chapter 8

During the next two hours, Ruth's condition took a turn for the worse. Her blood pressure skyrocketed and her strength plummeted. While the nurses worked diligently to stabilize her condition, the doctor raced in. She looked at Ruth's frail form lying on the bed, a fragment of the friend she had known for a very long time. As she watched Ruth teeter on the edge of consciousness, she had a very sick feeling in the pit of her stomach.

She turned to Brian, who was standing there with a look of terror on his face, his body trembling at the sight of his wife suffering so. "Listen to me, Brian," she said sternly, "we have a very touchy situation here. Your wife's condition has reached the very dangerous stages of toxemia. We're trying very hard to help her, but we can't get her blood pressure down. I'm afraid we have to do an emergency C-section right now to at least save the baby."

Immediately, she knew she had slipped and Brian caught on.

He looked at her, stunned, his lips quivering. "What do you mean—at least save the baby? Are you saying that my wife's going to die? Please don't tell me I have to choose between my wife and my baby?"

"No, that's not what I am saying," she said. "I didn't mean for it to come out that way. What I am saying is a C-section is the only chance that either of them has."

By now, Brian was bordering on hysteria. "Whatever it takes, just do it. But please, doctor, save my wife. She means everything to me. I can't imagine life without her."

"We'll do everything we can," she said as she turned away from him. Brian didn't see the tears running down her face, or the resignation in her eyes.

Dr. Urbanski gave a few orders to the nurses, and they quickly prepared Ruth's bed for transport. Within minutes, Ruth was being rushed through the operating room doors on the next floor of the hospital. The doctor urged Brian to remain outside, but he protested vehemently. "There's no way I'm staying out here while my wife and daughter are in there and could die!"

Against her better judgment, she conceded, "Alright. Just try to stay strong for Ruth. That's the most important thing that'll help her now."

Quickly, she ushered him inside the room and toward the corner, where a nurse was waiting to help him scrub properly and don one of their fashionable gowns. A minute later, he was standing next to his wife, trembling in fear amid a sea of green smocks and surgical instruments. His heart was beating heavily as grabbed Ruth's hand. Her eyelids fluttered for a second before opening and she smiled at him weakly.

"I'm here with you, dear," he said in his most reassuring voice, desperately hoping to hide the fear resonating within him.

She tried to respond, but her throat was dry and scratchy. Instead, she just mouthed the words, 'I love you.'

"I love you too, dear. More than you will ever know."

***

"Give me a break!" Nybbas said as he spat on the floor. Then, he put his arm around Michael's shoulder, the demon's touch sending a javelin of fire shooting through him. "As you can see, the situation has grown exponentially worse. Now comes the moment of truth, Michael. Say very dangerous complications were to arise that endangered both the life of the mother and the life of her unborn child, which would you choose to save? Keep in mind the hellish implications your decision will have."

Michael felt like his heart was about to burst. *How can I make a choice like this? No matter what I say, someone is going to die.* He felt the love that bound the couple together—a love that at one time he could relate to. But then he thought of the baby. How could he sacrifice her life before she even had a chance to live? He watched the scene before him unfold for a moment without answering.

Suddenly, a loud siren echoed through the room, along with the flashing of a red strobe light, which cast a sinister glow throughout. The nurses scrambled madly about, screaming hysterically as Dr. Urbanski rushed in, holding a chainsaw at her side, her eyes holding the look of a lunatic inside.

"Is she ready?" the doctor bellowed.

The nurses nodded a collective 'yes' as they huddled in the corner to escape the doctor's wrath.

The doctor peeled the gown back from Ruth's stomach to show the worm-thing pushing up through her skin, trying desperately to escape its prison.

Dr. Urbanski looked at Michael with a twinkle in her eye

and an evil grin on her face. "What'll it be, sport? The mother, or the baby?"

Michael looked at the feeble woman lying on the table with one foot already through death's door. Then he looked at the abomination trying to force its way into this world. The decision should've been easy. Save the woman. Kill the monstrosity.

Around him, the doctor revved the chainsaw louder, causing a chorus of screams to fly from the nurses, while she pressed him repeatedly, "What'll it be, sport? What'll it be sport? What'll it be sport?"

That little voice in the back of his mind, barely detectable, came to life again, and he had his answer. "Save the baby," he said.

A frown overcame the doctor's demented face for a second before the scene changed back to a normal operating room. Then Michael watched in amazement as a brilliant light filled the room directly above Ruth's head. A second later, a scene filled the light. Two angels stood before her, their gossamer wings shimmering rainbows. In their arms, they held a newborn baby, one supporting each side of the infant, and they presented the baby to her.

**

A feeling of peace engulfed Ruth as she looked at her daughter through eyes filled with tears. She turned toward Brian and cleared her throat so she could say the words that she knew would be her last. "Everything's going to be alright, Brian. I can see her! I see our daughter, and she's more beautiful than I could've imagined."

She smiled. "The angels are here with me now. They're going to look after our baby girl as she enters this world."

Brian's lips trembled. "You're going to be fine, Ruth. Please, don't talk like you're going to leave me."

Feebly, Ruth tried to raise her finger to her lips to silence him, but her hand just flopped back down to her side.

Dr. Urbanski stepped in. "It's time."

Brian nodded sadly.

The doctor motioned to a couple of the nurses and they lowered a screen onto Ruth's stomach to block her view.

Ruth cringed as Dr. Urbanski began the incision. She cleared her throat once more. "Be strong, dear, for Isabelle's sake. I've already had a wonderful life with you. Now it's her turn. Promise me you'll raise her to be the beautiful princess she's meant to be."

Tears streamed down his cheeks as he sought to control the anguish overwhelming him. His own throat became raspy as he struggled to find the strength to say those two words, for saying them meant he was releasing her from this life. Her hand squeezed his gently, and he resigned himself to honor her dying wish even though a part of him was dying at that very moment as well. "I promise," he mumbled softly, knowing it would be the last words she would ever hear.

Ruth smiled softly, her face an expression of peace and tranquility. Then she closed her eyes and died.

At that same moment, when the flame was extinguished from one angel's soul, it ushered another angel into this brave new world. Brian heard the cry issue from his baby Isabelle's lips, and a moment later he was holding his daughter in his arms. He didn't know how he was going to go on, but he would do everything he could to keep his promise to his wife.

Chapter 9

Gabriel jumped into the pond with a frenzied desperation. The water was thick and murky, and he felt an evil pulse emanating from its depths as he swam downward. Soon enough, a black mass came within view, writhing like a veil of shadows.

As Gabriel moved closer, the water around him came alive. Instantly he was overrun by a school of viscous creatures— fish-like beasts cross-bred between giant piranha and squid— that lunged at him on all sides. Glinting razor teeth gnashed at his flesh while barbed tentacles wrapped around him like relentless chains.

In desperation, Gabriel thrashed wildly against the slimy horde that surrounded him. He felt his strength ebbing as the monstrous creatures mercilessly yanked at him, dragging him deeper into the abyss. With a final burst of energy, he broke free and shot toward the curtain.

Just as he was about to pass through, a mammoth tentacle stretched up from the depths to ensnare him in its coils. There was nothing he could do as countless thick membranous ropes bound his body tightly and forced him downward, plummeting further into the unforgiving depths.

He finally crashed onto the jagged floor of a massive underwater cave, pinned down beneath the crushing weight of the colossal sea beast. Its eyes glinted wickedly in the darkness, mocking him.

A voice behind him drew his attention. As the tentacles withdrew into the watery darkness, he turned his head to find a tall, slender woman with fiery red hair and bright green eyes standing defiantly. "Gabriel! Nice of you to drop in!"

"Circe!" Gabriel exclaimed. "I should've known you were a part of this, witch!"

Circe feigned hurt. "Aren't you a little above name calling?"

"I don't know what game you're playing here, but whatever it is, you should be prepared to lose."

Circe laughed. "I see the angels are as arrogant as ever."

"No, just confident."

"Well, whatever you want to call it, just know that Belial doesn't like you sticking your nose into his business."

"That's kind of hard to do when he's trying to destroy the world."

"That's a little melodramatic, don't you think? Belial just wants what belongs to him. Nothing wrong with that."

"See, that's where our opinion differs. Nothing was taken from Belial. He gave up his place in Heaven when he followed Lucifer."

"That's just a matter of perspective."

Gabriel looked at her steadily. "It seems we're at an impasse, then."

Circe cocked her head to one side for a second in thought. "That, it does." She brought her hands up quickly and a bolt of energy shot out of them toward Gabriel.

Gabriel wheeled around, avoiding the blast, his sword

appearing in his hand with a flash. He roared and lunged forward, his blade cutting through the air in an arc that sliced Circe across her arm. She screamed in agony, and with a wave of her hand, the rocky ceiling above them came crashing down on Gabriel's leg, pinning him to the ground.

"Stop this, Circe!" he shouted. "Belial is deceiving you! Don't trust him, he's only looking for power."

"He's nothing but a pawn in my plans," she spat contemptuously, before releasing a flurry of energy blasts towards Gabriel.

Gabriel quickly pulled himself up from the rubble, only to be knocked back by the first wave. He quickly steadied himself and raced towards her. With lightning-fast reflexes, he deflected each projectile away from him while slashing at Circe with his blade. As she stumbled backward, Gabriel lunged forward and seconds later, the tip of his sword dug deep into her stomach.

"I tried to warn you Circe," he said sadly as he watched icy hatred fill her eyes. "It didn't have to be like this."

Her mouth drawn into a snarl of rage, Circe growled out one last warning before a tentacle from the sea-beast grabbed Gabriel and yanked him toward the water. When he looked back at where Circe had fallen, there was nothing but emptiness.

Chapter 10

Nybbas looked at Michael with an irritated look on his face as he held Abaddon in his arms. "This fucker's stronger than I thought. I can see why Belial's getting frustrated. Nonetheless, I don't think he can take much more. What do you think, Abaddon? Another shot maybe?"

Abaddon gave a soft meow before she opened her mouth and the tentacles shot forward to embed into Michael's skull once more.

***

Peter sat at his desk in front of a dual-monitor computer setup wearing a wireless headset, with a video camera mounted on a small tripod sitting off to the side recording him. One monitor depicted an open-world video game, while the other was a split-screen with Peter's face on one side and a chat room message board on the other. Messages scrolled across the screen as Peter started the live-stream of his game play.

"Are you guys ready to kick some ass?" He said enthusiastically.

The comments in the chat room started scrolling in. Peter took a moment to read a few of them and chuckled.

"Just start the game already, Dude," one of the on-line players said through the headset.

Peter replied, "Okay, okay. Hold your horses."

The player responded, "Who says that anymore?"

Peter laughed. "Hey, this is my stream. I can say whatever I want."

"Whatever."

As soon as the game sparked to life, Peter was pulled into a vortex of gaming bliss. Just as he was about to reach his peak level of concentration, the lights flickered ominously and his screens went black.

"No! Not now!" Peter screamed, his voice echoing in the dead silence. As he waited anxiously for the monitors to flicker back to life, a breathless eternity seemed to pass. Finally, the screens crackled with energy and his game resumed. His heart racing, Peter breathed easier when he saw that nothing from his game had been lost.

"What the hell was that?" the other player asked. "I lost you, dude."

"Beats the hell out of me?" Peter replied. "I lost power for a second."

"You almost fucked the whole game up for us. Try not to let that happen again."

"That's a little dramatic, don't you think? Besides, it's not like I had any control over it."

Peter read through some comments from the chat room and stopped cold when he read one that asked, *Who's that standing behind you?*

"Haha, very funny, guys," Peter retorted. "You're not gonna get me that easy."

Peter's fingers moved with lightning speed as he returned

to his game and navigated through the virtual world, his eyes fixed on the screen in front of him. Suddenly, Peter froze in terror when a powerful jolt shook his chair from behind. He sat there motionless for a moment, his heart pounding in his chest. Slowly turning his head, he saw Simba, his Calico cat, rubbing up against the back of his chair.

"What are you doing down there?" Peter growled in irritation. "You're distracting me from my game."

Simba replied with a short 'meow' as he brushed against Peter's leg.

Turning back to his game, Peter froze again when he saw Simla in front of him, sleeping soundly on the opposite edge of the desk. Panic set in as he looked back down at the creature on the floor, its fur slick with an oily residue that dripped onto the carpet. Suddenly, it exploded into a demonic shapeless thing with fangs and claws before vanishing.

In one swift movement, Peter ripped off his headset as a deafening squelch pierced his ears. His heart was racing as he realized that the line between fantasy and reality had been brutally shattered.

"What the fuck!?" he cried.

He glanced at the screen and the words, *Behind You!* scrolled repeatedly from those in the chat room.

A loud and thunderous breath echoed off the walls of Peter's room, causing him to jump. The hairs on the back of his neck stood up like needles as a sharp chill ran down his spine. His eyes widened in horror as he saw a large, dark shadow looming over him, its outstretched claws dripping with an unknown evil energy.

Simba jumped up and let out an angry hiss towards the figure, snapping Peter out of his terror, and when he looked back again, the shadow was gone.

Peter stumbled out of the room in terror, flailing his arms wildly until he reached the living room where he tripped over the edge of the couch with a loud crash. He scrambled to his feet and dashed out the front door, gasping for air as he leaned against his car. A sudden dread ran through his bones as he glimpsed a dark silhouette passing by his bedroom window from inside.

"Holy shit!" he gasped as he pulled his phone from his pocket and dialed 911 with trembling fingers.

A half-hour later, Peter watched anxiously as the two police officers walked out of his house empty-handed.

"Did you find anyone inside?" Peter asked.

The first officer shook his head. "No. We searched the place thoroughly."

"I swear there was someone there!"

The second officer replied, "Well, whoever it was is gone."

"So, what now?"

"The precinct's just down the road. We can be here in a couple minutes if you need us again."

Peter's eyes darted nervously as he watched the police car drive away until its taillights disappeared into the night. With a heavy sigh, he trudged his way back toward his house. The dread engulfing him made it feel like he was walking through quicksand.

That night, Peter lay in bed with the covers pulled up to his chin, wide-eyed and scanning the room for any sign of danger. When Simba jumped up on the bed, Peter felt his body tense as a chill ran down his spine, and memories of the demon cat flashed back in his mind before he reluctantly extended a hand toward the feline.

But instead of turning off the light next to his bed like he planned, he left it on, unable to face the darkness alone.

The shrill sound of the alarm clock the next morning woke

Peter from a fitful sleep. His arm moved woodenly to stop the noise, but just as quickly froze in midair when he heard a deep rumble coming from below. Peering down at his chest he saw Simba curled up and sleeping atop him like an anvil, trapping him into place. "Ugh! Simba," he muttered angrily, "you're getting too fat for this."

Simba responded with a soft meow.

"You need to get off so I can get ready for work," he said as he tried to squirm out from under the cat.

Reluctantly, Simba jumped from his chest and scampered out of the room. Peter sighed as he turned off the alarm and rolled out of bed.

Minutes later, Peter stood under the shower, letting the water cascade over him, trying to wash away the darkness of the night before. He was startled suddenly by a whisper-like breath on his ear. His heart raced as he quickly glanced around the room, but it was empty.

Just when he thought he was safe, he felt a chill lingering in the air and a sense of dread that he had experienced the previous night began to creep back into his mind. He hurriedly dried himself off and brushed his teeth, only to notice a dark shadow figure hovering over him in the mirror as he lowered his head to spit out the toothpaste. When he looked up again, the figure was gone, leaving Peter trembling in fear.

Chapter 11

Mary walked along the small bridge spanning the width of a small pond in the center of the park as an assortment of joggers and bikers passed her.

Warm sunlight glittered off the tiny ripples on the water, causing them to sparkle like diamonds. Mary leaned forward and peered into the pond. The sounds of children laughing and playing echoed through the nearby trees. Her face sobered as her thoughts drifted back to her own childhood. There was a distinct sadness in her eyes as she longed for better times that now seemed like such distant memories.

As Mary looked down, the pond met her gaze, engulfing her in its tranquility. A large splash suddenly broke the stillness, and as the water split, a savage creature, its face long and disfigured, stared up at her with an evil grin.

Mary gasped, her heart racing while she tried to steady herself on the bridge's railing. Her breathing quickened as she watched the creature swim around the pond, its eyes never leaving her.

Suddenly, the creature lunged out of the water towards her, its mouth gaping open to reveal rows of razor-sharp teeth. She let out a scream as she tried to stumble backwards, but her foot caught on a large stone and sent her tumbling. Her arms flailed frantically as she started to plummet over the railing into the jaws of the beast.

Suddenly, a hand reached out and grabbed her. She was surprised to see Dr. Samuel there dressed in a tie-dye t-shirt and sweat pants.

"Dr. Samuel!" she cried as she looked around frantically with a terrified look on her face. "Where is it?"

"Where is what?" Dr. Samuel replied.

"You didn't see that thing jump out at me?"

She glanced nervously at the water and was shocked to see all evidence of the demon gone.

"I'm sorry," he said. "I didn't see anything."

"What're you doing here?" she said as she caught her breath.

Dr. Samuel replied, "Besides saving you from a mysterious creature attack and a nasty fall? I come here on my days off to relax. Nature helps me get my mind away from all the clinical stuff for a little bit."

"I didn't mean it like that. I just meant that it's a pretty big coincidence that you came along when you did."

Dr. Samuel smiled at her. "As a man of science, I really don't believe in coincidence. Every moment in life happens for a reason."

"Are you saying we don't have free will?"

"No, not at all. I'm merely suggesting that every moment happens because of past moments. Our present actions shape our future possibilities."

"That's pretty deep."

Dr. Samuel chuckled. "I guess it is."

Mary glanced back down at the water nervously. The face was gone, but a small group of bubbles sat on the top of the water in its place.

Dr. Samuel watched Mary with a look of concern on his face. "How's Michael doing, by the way?"

Mary was silent for a moment, then shrugged. "Don't know? I haven't seen him since he ran out of your office."

"I'm sorry," Dr. Samuel replied. "Hopefully, he's okay."

"Some weird guy came to my apartment. Said he was a friend of Michael's and that he was okay. The guy was kinda creepy, though."

A look of concern crept into Dr. Samuel's eyes for a moment. "I'm a good judge of character, and I can tell that Michael's a strong man with a good heart. He'll pull through whatever he's dealing with."

"I just wish he wouldn't push me away all the time," Mary said.

"He either feels like he's protecting you, or that he doesn't deserve your help, or love, for that matter."

"But that's ridiculous! It's just the opposite. He needs to realize that we're stronger together."

Sr. Samuel put his hand on her shoulder. "Just be patient with him and be there when he needs you the most."

Mary looked at him sadly. "I'm so tired, Doc. I don't know if I can?"

Dr. Samuel watched as Mary walked away, then turned and looked at the water with a concerned look on his face. The demon face materialized once more for a brief second, scoffing up at him, then disappeared.

Chapter 12

Thunder rumbled overhead before tiny raindrops sprinkled on Peter while he ran to his car, streaks of lightning signaling the approaching storm. Off in the distance, the rain came down hard and heavy, as if an invisible hand was pouring out buckets of water onto the landscape.

Then, in a matter of seconds, the drops grew in size, turning quickly to a light downpour as Peter pulled his keys from his pocket. A flash of lightning, this time much closer, caused him to jump before he pressed the button to unlock his door. Nothing happened. After several tries, he put the key in the cylinder to unlock it manually, but it wouldn't budge. Something was stuck inside the keyhole. He bent down to inspect the lock and saw a tiny pebble lodged inside.

"What in the world? How am I supposed to get to work now?"

After trying to pull the object out of the lock cylinder unsuccessfully, he started to walk around to the other side of the car when the door suddenly popped open.

A gust of wind pelted Peter in the face as he raced for the door and climbed inside. He sat there for a second shaking from both the cold and the increasing dread that was festering inside of him. Then he put the key in the ignition and turned it, only to be met with silence.

"You gotta be shitting me! What in the hell is going on here?"

Peter jumped a second later when a large hairy spider crawled from under the dash, brushing up against his hand, and scurried up to disappear into the blower vent, sending another shudder coursing through him.

He shook off a wave of revulsion and tried the key once more. This time, he was startled when a jolt of static electricity sprung out and struck his fingers.

"Ouch!" he yelled, jerking back before examining his finger; there was a small scorch mark where the current had made contact. After an anxious pause, he slowly extended his arm again toward the console, hesitantly laying his burned finger on the key before turning it. The engine sputtered, trying to turn the car over with all the vigor of a dying sloth. All he heard was an agonizingly slow creaking sound that threatened to break his last bit of hope.

Peter growled in frustration as he slammed his hand onto the steering wheel. "Come on! I can't afford for you to give up on me now!"

As if he hoped his feeble prayer would influence his transportation problem, Peter turned the key one more time, muttering to himself, "Come on, baby. You can do it."

The car's engine groaned in objection as Peter pounded the dashboard with his fist, determined to get it started. Finally, after an eternity of grinding, the engine sputtered to life and a patch of black smoke emerged from under the hood, writhing in the air like some dark spirit before vanishing into the atmosphere.

Peter sat there for a moment, afraid to move. Then suddenly, the sun burst through the clouds, blasting him with its hellish rays that shone directly through his windshield. He yanked his sun visor down to avoid being temporarily blinded by the glare.

He glanced at his watch and frowned. "Jackson's gonna have my ass if I'm late!"

He could still make it if, by some miracle, he hit every green light through town. With a sense of urgency, Peter pushed the car faster than ever before, hoping she still had enough life left in her to make it in one piece.

Minutes later, Peter pulled into a parking space and jumped out of his car. He slung his backpack over his shoulder and ran toward the front entrance of the building, tripping as he bounded over the curb, and fell to the sidewalk. "Ow! Shit!"

His hand brushed against a large, black spider as he pushed himself to his knees. He cringed as it scurried away into the grass. "What the hell is going on here?"

A hand reached out to him. "Here, let me help you up."

Peter looked up to see Nybbas standing there wearing a sport coat. As he accepted his hand, he suddenly got dizzy and staggered for a second before he steadied himself.

"You okay there?" Nybbas asked.

"Yeah, just stood up too fast."

"Ah, Orthostatic Hypotension. A sudden drop in blood pressure when a person stands up."

Peter looked at Nybbas questioningly. "Are you a doctor?"

Nybbas chuckled. "No. But I play one on TV."

"I knew you looked familiar! You were Dr. Sullivan on that hospital show a long time ago."

"E.R 911, Manhattan, and it wasn't that long ago."

Peter flushed, "Sorry, I didn't mean any disrespect."

"None taken," Nybbas said with a smile.

"Are you a client here?"

"Not yet. I'm still looking at options to expand my marketing efforts for a clothing line I'm working on."

"Well, Jasper & Associates is one of the top marketing firms in the area."

Nybbas looked thoughtful for a moment. "I'll keep that in mind. In the meantime, I'm sure I'm keeping you from your job."

Peter looked at his watch. "Shit! Sorry, I have to go."

"No problem," Nybbas said with a smile. "Who knows? Maybe I'll be seeing you around?"

Peter nodded and started walking toward the door.

Nybbas called out, "Oh, and Peter, you really shouldn't have such a negative view of spiders. They're actually one of the most beneficial creatures on this planet."

Peter stopped and turned around, but Nybbas was gone. A slight tingle wound through Peter's brain, adding to the growing darkness invading his being as he entered the front door to the building.

Sandy, the short and fiery receptionist, snickered as he walked by.

"Hi, Sandy," he smiled.

"Cutting it a little close today, aren't we, Pete?" She chided.

"Hey, I'm here with a minute to spare."

"That's just enough time to put your stuff away and head to Jackson's office. He's waiting for you, and he seems kinda pissed."

"That's not good. Any idea what it's about?"

"Beats me? But hopefully you can pull the stick out of his ass so he's not a total dick all day."

Peter chuckled, "I'll see what I can do. By the way, did you see the guy from that emergency TV show that was in here a few minutes ago?"

Sandy looked at him blankly.

"He played Dr. Sullivan?" Peter said. "E.R. 911?"

Sandy replied, "Peter, there hasn't been anyone in or out of here for the last half hour."

"But I just saw him."

"I don't know what to tell you, Peter? Now, you better get to Jackson's office or he's really gonna get pissed."

With an uneasy look on his face, Peter turned and walked down the hall.

He hurried to his desk to drop off his coat and then proceeded down the hall to Mr. Jackson's office, taking a moment to admire the Information & Security Manager placard on the wall next to the door. *Some day*, he thought wistfully.

A soft knock on the door was enough to alert his boss, and he was greeted by a deep, stern voice a second later, "Come in."

Peter stepped into the office, just as Mr. Jackson was tapping a series of commands on a keyboard in front of him, all while mumbling under his breath.

"Good, Peter, you're here. Something's come up that needs your attention."

"What's going on?"

"Rebecca downloaded a virus onto her computer when she clicked on an e-mail attachment."

Peter rolled his eyes. "Shit! She knows better than that."

"I know. Apparently, she thought the e-mail was from someone she knew. It completely wiped out her hard drive."

"What do you need me to do?" Peter asked.

"I've already re-routed the networks around the server that Rebecca's computer was connected to. I need you to check out that server to see if it's infected as well. Then I need you to replace the hard drive in her computer and restore her system. After that, you can re-educate her on the fundamentals of safe e-mail practices."

"No problem. It shouldn't take too long to get everything back in order."

Peter turned to leave and stopped.

"Is there something else, Peter?" Mr. Jackson asked.

"I was wondering if you had a chance to go over my review yet? I've been putting a lot of extra work in lately and was hoping it might reflect in my performance appraisal?"

"In other words, you're asking me if you're getting a raise?"

Peter looked flustered. "I...I didn't mean it like that. I was asking about my performance. And if it's acceptable, then a raise would be nice."

Mr. Jackson rose from his seat and towered over Peter, standing nearly seven feet tall. His face grew long and sinister. A wide, toothy grin spread across his lips. "You've got guts, kid, coming in here like this and asking for something you don't deserve. Do you have any idea how easy it is to find another sniveling, worthless little nerd to take your place?"

Peter's lips quivered as Mr. Jackson pulled a multi-tool from his desk and opened it up, revealing a long, sharp blade. "I've half a mind to shove this knife through your balls and split you in two from groin to Adam's apple."

Peter backed away from the desk and his foot slipped on something. He was horrified to see a puddle of blood beneath his feet and saw Sandy slumped against the wall in the corner with her eyes plucked out. He opened his mouth to scream.

Chapter 13

Mr. Jackson's voice snapped Peter back to the present. "Is there something else, Peter?"

Peter turned around in confusion and saw Mr. Jackson sitting at his desk normally. His voice came out in a stutter, "No...no, that's it."

"Keep me updated on your progress."

"Will do," Peter replied as he left the office on the verge of panic, working hard to suppress his terror.

As soon as he was out of the office, Peter leaned against the wall next to the door shaking visibly. His heart raced and his lungs burned as a wave of anxiety threatened to crash over him. He tried to tell himself it was just exhaustion from working too hard lately, but he knew it was more than that.

He took a few deep breaths to calm himself before trudging slowly down the hall, still muttering to himself, "I've just been working too hard. That's all it is. It's finally catching up with me." Although he wanted desperately to believe what he said was true, he felt like inescapable doom was lurking around every corner.

After a quick trip to his office to grab his equipment, he stopped at the door to the server room and passed his keycard over a panel on the wall.

After setting his backpack on the floor, he grabbed the handle on the front of the server and pulled it forward out of the array. As he crouched down to unzip his backpack, his finger got caught in the teeth of the zipper, cutting the end of it. "Ow! Shit!"

He shook his hand for a few seconds and then sucked on the end of his finger to stop the flow of blood. "This day just keeps getting better every minute."

Peter pulled his laptop out and plugged one side of a braided cord into the side of it. He was about to plug the other end into a port on the server when a large, black spider, identical to the one in his car earlier, and after that, on the sidewalk outside, scurried out from under the motherboard.

He jumped back and nearly dropped his laptop as he banged into the cooling unit behind him on the wall. A cry flew from his lips when his elbow hit the edge of the metal casing and cut a large gash in his arm. "Oh my God! What the hell?"

As a stream of blood dripped onto the floor, Peter looked around the room for anything he might use to staunch the wound. Finding nothing useful, he scavenged through his backpack with his other hand and pulled out a small, crumpled tissue. He pressed it against the cut, wincing at the sharp pain shooting up his arm. The spider was nowhere to be seen, but Peter couldn't shake the feeling that the spider was following him, stalking him.

He shook his head, trying to clear his thoughts, and turned back to his laptop. He plugged the cord into the server port, and after a moment of waiting, a small window popped up on his screen. He grinned, relieved that he had managed to make the connection. His grin turned into a frown when he ran the diagnostic and found the server hard drive corrupted.

"Shit! I was afraid of that."

He powered down the server and quickly installed a new hard drive. When Peter pressed a button on his laptop to format the new drive, the screen on his laptop glitched, and for a brief second, almost imperceptible, an evil face sneered at him. Then the screen steadied.

He watched nervously as the progress bar on the screen filled up, only to stop at ninety-nine percent. "Oh, come on! Don't do this to me!"

After an agonizing minute, the screen blinked a couple of times and then the formatting finally completed, allowing Peter to breathe a little easier.

"Thank God!" he said, relieved that something had finally gone right this morning.

Peter's hands flew over the keyboard as he typed in a few commands. He then disconnected his laptop and quickly shoved it back into his bag before sliding the server back in place. When he reached for the door handle, something suddenly pulled on his backpack and nearly yanked him off balance, causing him to cry out in panic. His heart raced as he ran from the room, desperately trying to find freedom from whatever unseen force was haunting him.

Minutes later, he reached Rebecca's workstation and found her sitting quietly at her desk with a broken look on her face. Tears still lingered in her eyes and her glasses sat next to an open Bible on her desk. Her dark hair had come undone from its tight bun and lay scattered around her shoulders.

Peter did his best to cheer her up, "Don't worry, Rebecca, everything's gonna be fine. All of your data is backed up daily on multiple servers, so I should be able to have you good as new in no time."

She looked at him through her red eyes. "What did Mr. Jackson say? Am I going to be fired?"

Peter chuckled, "Fired? You? No way! They're not going to fire the nicest person here. I wouldn't let them. But you have to promise me something, though."

"What's that?"

"That you won't open up any more e-mail attachments, okay?"

"I promise."

"Good. Now let's fix this computer so you can get back to work."

"It makes me sad and angry," she said. "Whoever did this used scripture to create something so horrible."

"That's how bad people operate," Peter responded. "They take advantage of the inherent goodness in others and exploit it."

"Well, it's terrible."

"I know," Peter said as he recalled his own personal experiences; from his grandparents being milked out of thousands of dollars in a health-care scam; his best friend having her identity stolen; to even his own experience when he went into business with a friend of his, only to have them disappear with all of his cash.

He sighed. "All we can do is keep plugging away, day after day, and hope that at some point the world becomes a better place to live in."

As he crouched down to disconnect her workstation, Peter felt a soft burst of air on his ear, like an unspoken whisper. He glanced over his shoulder, but Rebecca was leaning against the far wall of her cubicle, giving him room to work.

Shrugging it off as his imagination, he pulled a small screwdriver from his back pocket. As soon as the tip of the blade touched the screw on the case, another jolt of static electricity rifled through him. This time, it was enough to send a flurry of dancing lights through his brain for a second before everything went dark.

***

When Peter's senses returned, he found himself strapped to a chair in a small room with a large monitor covering the wall in front of him. He heard a low moan at his feet and looked down to see a man lying there, his arms and face bruised and bleeding. His hair was matted with blood and a dark, haunted look filled his eyes as he opened them and sat up.

"Where are we, and what's going on here?" Peter asked as he squirmed to get out of his restraints.

"I have a pretty good idea about both, and you're not going to like them," Michael replied.

"Who are you?"

"My name is Michael, and I'm afraid we're trapped in Hell, or at least a version of it."

"Wherever we are, Michael, just get me the fuck out of this!"

"Calm down. Panicking right now won't help. What's your name?"

"It's Peter."

"Okay, Peter. I'm going to try to get these restraints off you."

Michael got to his knees and began to work at Peter's restraints, but as soon as he touched them, the monitor on the wall lit up and Nybbas' image filled the screen. "I wouldn't do that if I were you," the demon said. "Take a closer look."

Michael crouched down and was shocked to see a taught wire attached to the back of Peter's chair that was hooked through the restraint that wrapped around his chest. His eyes followed the wire as it traversed along the baseboard of the wall behind the chair to the corner of the connecting wall, and then up toward the ceiling. An eyelet embedded in the drywall carried the wire toward the center of the ceiling directly above the chair, where it was held tight to a trigger attached to a large ax mounted on a swivel. Any disturbance would send the blade rushing downward toward Peter's chest.

"What do you want, Nybbas?" Michael said.

Peter exclaimed, "I know this guy! I saw him outside my work earlier today."

"Hello, Peter," Nybbas said. "See, I told you we'd be seeing each other again."

"What the fuck is going on here?" Peter asked, the terror rising in his voice.

Nybbas replied, "The two of you are going to play a game. And the outcome may very well decide the future of the entire world. Have you heard of escape rooms? They're all the rage right now. And I've cooked up a pretty juicy one. Michael, you have ten minutes to save Peter from being sliced in two. Have fun!"

Nybbas' image disappeared and was immediately replaced with a large countdown timer that filled the whole screen.

Michael stood there in shock for a second, unmoving.

"This isn't real, is it?" Peter cried.

"I don't know what's real anymore. But from past experience, we can't just assume this is some nightmare we'll wake up from."

"Then you need to figure this thing out as fast as possible!"

Michael looked quickly around for anything that might give him a clue. He'd never experienced an escape room before, but he'd heard guys at work talk about them, so he kind of knew the basics. The trick was finding that first clue.

The room was sparsely furnished with only a bookshelf against one wall, and a roll-top desk along the opposite. A keyhole was embedded in the wall right in front of them below the monitor. The lack of a door or window was disconcerting. *How the fuck did we even get there in the first place?* But Michael already knew that the rules of logic no longer applied.

"Try the desk!" Peter suggested.

Michael raced over and tried to push the roll-top open, but it was locked, along with all the drawers. "Shit! There's got to be a key in here somewhere!"

He ran to the bookshelf and felt along the top, hoping to get lucky. A loud squeal erupted when he brushed against a large rat upset that it had been disturbed from its hiding place. "Ouch!" Michael cried as the vermin chomped down on his hand before it scurried into the shadows. Then he heard a tiny 'ping' like something metal had fallen to the floor.

"What happened?" Peter asked nervously.

"A fucking rat bit me! But I think I heard something drop."

Michael searched the floor behind the bookshelf, laying down on his side and stretching his arm as far as he could reach, praying desperately that the savage animal had vanished for good. Then his fingers wrapped around something metallic and he brought out a small silver key.

He rushed to the desk and quickly inserted the key just as the counter reached seven minutes. Beneath the roll-top was a red button encased in glass mounted to the top of the desk with the words 'In case of emergency, break glass' etched in red letters. A small hammer lay next to the glass, inviting him to use it. Michael's first impulse was to break the glass and press the button immediately. But, knowing the demon's tendencies, he waited until he knew for sure that was the best course of action.

Frustration began to bubble when he tried the drawers in

the desk, but found them still locked. Maybe the red button actually was the answer, and his indecision had cost them precious seconds? Without further hesitation, he picked up the hammer and smashed the glass. Immediately, the top right drawer of the desk popped open. The only item in the drawer was a small, portable metal detector. Michael picked it up and turned it over in his hands in confusion.

"Just focus on finding the other key," Peter implored. "What kind of books are on the shelf?"

Michael sorted through the spines of the titles quickly, trying his best to figure out which one could be hiding a secret. This was the moment when he wished he'd tried harder in school. Maybe then he'd understand what he was looking at? The titles were a mishmash of seemingly unrelated material. There were scientific manuals dealing with quantum physics and molecular biology intermingled with classics such as 'Huckleberry Finn' and 'Little Women',

"These don't make any sense!" Michael said.

The timer reached five minutes and Nybbas' voice blasted through the room from hidden speakers somewhere overhead, "Five minutes left! I repeat, that's five minutes left!"

"Read the titles off!" Peter said.

Michael craned his neck sideways so he could read the spines clearly, "Murder on the Orient Express, Introduction to Quantum Physics, Charlotte's Web, Huckleberry Finn, A Time to Die, Encyclopedia of Anatomy, Little Women, Samurai, Beginner's Guide to Astrology, Othello, Dante's Inferno, and Year of the Dragon. Like I said, there's no rhyme or reason!"

"There has to be a reason," Peter cried. "They wouldn't be there if they weren't important. We're running out of time! We have to think!"

As the timer reached four minutes, Peter suddenly exclaimed, "It's an anagram! What do the first letters of the books spell?"

Michael looked again at each title and his mouth grew dry as his stomach churned. "They spell Michaels Body," he said sadly.

Peter's eyes grew wide, "The key is inside you? What kind of sick fuck does something like that?"

"You have no idea."

Michael looked at the timer sadly. Three minutes left.

He took a deep breath to try to quiet the tempest swirling in his brain, but it was no use. The storm didn't have any inclination of letting down. He resigned himself to do whatever was necessary to save Peter, and that resignation gave him a sliver of strength, enough at least to pick up the metal detector and turn it on.

Slowly, he passed the apparatus over his body, starting at his head and chest, and then moving it over each arm. When he got to his abdomen, the wand started beeping. He moved slowly around, trying to pinpoint the location, and stopped when it became a steady beep on his lower left side.

Pressing his left thumb into his side to mark the spot, he dropped the wand and rushed over to retrieve the anatomy book from the shelf. Frantically, he flipped through the pages with his free hand, trying to find any reference he could use so he didn't end up killing himself in the process. But the words and diagrams became blurry as he looked at them. Sweat began to drip from his brow, and his face felt flush. Then he remembered the rat.

He glanced at his right hand and saw that the wound had swelled and was oozing yellow puss. Realizing they were both running out of time, he dropped the book and rushed back to the desk. He knew there was only way he could do this, and he prayed he had the strength to see it through.

Two minutes left.

Michael quickly stripped his shirt off and rolled it tight before placing it between his teeth. Then he grabbed a broken piece of glass from the desk. The first cut sent a wave of pain searing through his brain and a fountain of blood draining down his leg to the floor. He tried to press his fingers inside, but the cut hadn't gone deep enough to penetrate all the way through his epidermis. He almost blacked out when he made the second cut, focusing with all his might to stay conscious for both of their sakes.

As the blood continued to flow like a river down his body, he pressed his fingers into his side once again. Amongst the slippery and soft tissue of his flesh and organs, his finger touched on something hard. His vision continued to blur and his brain felt like it was on fire as he tried to grasp the object.

Suddenly, he felt a coolness course through him and the fire in his brain calmed. His first thought was he had died and was no longer victim to the tortures he had endured. But then he realized that a gentle hand was guiding his. He gave a slight tug and pulled the bloody key from his body.

One minute left.

Michael ripped the shirt from mouth and pressed it onto his side to staunch the flow of blood, as he stumbled toward the wall. His knees buckled while he grew weaker with each passing second, and as his trembling hand reached forward to insert the key into the keyhole, it slipped out of his fingers and clanged to the floor.

Thirty seconds to go.

He dropped to his knees and fished through the puddle of blood on the floor until he felt the key.

Ten seconds to go.

With his last gasp, Michael reached up and inserted the

key into the slot. A loud click reverberated through the room as the countdown stopped with three seconds left. He breathed a sigh of relief that quickly turned to a gasp when the timer resumed, counting down. Two...One...Zero.

Michael watched in terror as the trigger released the ax from its perch on the ceiling. As it swung swiftly toward Peter's chest, a trapdoor under his chair suddenly sprang open and Peter plunged into the darkness below a split-second before the ax embedded itself into the wall directly behind where he had just been sitting.

Thankful that Peter's life had been spared, or at least he hoped so, Michael drifted off into unconsciousness.

Chapter 14

"Are you okay down there?" Rebecca asked, ripping Peter back to the present.

He bumped his head on the underside of her desk as he scooted out from underneath. The side of her computer case lay resting against the back wall, and he had her hard drive in his hand, although he didn't remember removing it.

"I saw a little spark under there and was afraid you'd gotten shocked," Rebecca continued.

Peter's brain was a fog. He had no recollection of the events he had suffered only a moment ago, and it felt like it had been ages ago when he had crawled under the desk to fix her computer, but in reality, it had only been a couple minutes. Something was lurking in the back of his mind, like a shadow waiting for the dark to arrive so it could unleash its nightmarish assault. He tried to pull it out into the open, but he couldn't quite grasp it.

"I'm okay," he replied. "Give me a few minutes and I'll have you back in business."

Rebecca nodded and moved aside.

After installing a new hard drive, Peter put the side panel back on her computer and nervously brought his screwdriver out. His hands were shaky as he touched the tip to the first screw. He breathed a little easier when nothing happened.

He booted the computer back up and typed a couple of commands on the keyboard to connect to the server. A few minutes later, her computer was good as new.

"Thank you, Peter," Rebecca said. "I don't know what we'd do without you around here?"

Peter smiled. "Maybe you could tell Jackson to give me a raise, then?"

Rebecca chuckled.

A flashback of Mr. Jackson threatening to gut him in half suddenly flew into Peter's head. "Scratch that," he said. "Probably better to stay clear of him for a bit."

Rebecca nodded and lowered her head as Peter grabbed his bag and left her cubicle.

Back at his desk, Peter's fingers danced across the keyboard as he tried to focus on his work, but his mind kept wandering to that nagging feeling. He knew something was off, but he couldn't figure out what it was. Suddenly, flashes of terrifying images overwhelmed him: Simba morphing into a demonic feline; shadowy figures lurking in his home; his car engulfed in a cloud of hellish smoke; and Sandy's lifeless body lying in a pool of blood with her eyes gouged out. Suddenly, a violent shiver swarmed through him when he remembered the escape room.

His brain felt like it was about to implode from the onslaught of these haunting visions. He wanted nothing more than to run away from it all, but he couldn't ignore the dark sense of foreboding that filled him up from the inside every time he stopped to think.

Finally, unable to bear it anymore, Peter dragged himself away from his desk and shuffled down the hall. When he returned to Rebecca's cubicle, he found her sitting at her desk with her Bible open again and reading intently. She didn't notice him at first, so he knocked lightly against the partition that separated her from the other workstations.

"Sorry," she said shyly. "I got caught up reading. Is something else wrong?"

"No. You're good. I just was wondering if I could borrow your Bible for a bit?"

Rebecca had all but forgotten about the incident earlier and was back to her usual bubbly self. "Sure, Peter," she replied enthusiastically. "Is there anything in particular I could help you with?"

"I was interested in the same passage you had it opened to earlier."

She thought about it for a minute. "Oh, you mean Revelations. It's a tough book to understand. We just started studying it in church."

"I was just curious to read it. Maybe it'll get me in the mood to go to church again."

Rebecca's smile brightened. "Take all the time you need."

She handed the Bible to Peter, and as soon as he touched it, an image of a computer screen flew into his head. It showed Psalms 23 scrolling slowly up the screen until the last line of the passage disappeared. A peal of devious laughter spewed from the speakers just before the screen went black.

Peter shuddered as the vision faded. After a quick 'thank you', he trudged back down through the hall, seeking answers to the horrors that had consumed him.

At his office, Peter feverishly pored over scripture until his head ached from comprehension. The words swirled around his mind like a maelstrom of confusion, and he felt utterly out of his depth. In the end, he humbly concluded that the Book of Revelations was something far beyond his reach.

Finally, with darkness descending on the city, Peter

reluctantly tucked the bible away and extinguished the light in his office with a heavy heart as he left.

As Peter pulled into a parking space outside of the small bank, he looked up through the windshield to see dark storm clouds quickly filling the sky.

"Looks like a bad storm's coming," he said somberly.

The car radio squelched for a second before he turned his car off. With a worried look in his eyes, he got out of his car and glanced all around. Thunder and lightning started attacking from all sides. "Apparently, it's already here," he said as his feeling of dread grew even darker.

Peter's heart pounded as he shuffled into the bank just minutes before closing. The tellers glared at him with obvious contempt, their faces twisted in frustration as customers continued to trickle in.

As he stood in line, Peter watched as a teller snapped at Rebecca, who was rummaging through her purse at the counter. "Do you need more time?" the teller spat, eyes darting towards the clock on the wall. "We're trying to close up here."

Rebecca's face flushed with embarrassment as she apologized and rifled through her belongings. The teller rolled her eyes impatiently, clearly irritated.

Peter looked around the room and suddenly felt trapped in another nightmare. As he neared the front of the line, he could feel the tension building around him like a living thing, ready to consume them all.

Suddenly, it hit him—this was no ordinary bank visit. Something far more sinister lurked beneath the surface. He could feel it. And he was caught right in the middle of it. Again.

"I'm sorry. I know it's here somewhere."

Finally, Rebecca found her check and handed it to the

Teller. With a grunt, the girl snatched the paper from her and slid it through the slot on her terminal.

Peter watched Rebecca with a sad look on his face as she struggled at the counter. Suddenly, he noticed a man wearing a long gray trench coat edging towards the counter. He tensed, every nerve in his body alert as the man slowly reached inside his coat and pulled out a gun. The room seemed to freeze as the man waved it around menacingly.

"Everybody down on the ground, now!" the man yelled.

The crowd stood paralyzed for a moment before everyone scrambled to the floor amidst a chorus of cries and screams.

Rebecca, in a state of panic, knocked over her purse, spilling its contents all over the counter. Without thinking, she nervously started stuffing everything back in.

The man lunged forward and grabbed Rebecca by her wrist, his fingers like vise grips. He brought the gun up to her head with a menacing glint in his eye. "I said get down, bitch!" he bellowed. His hand quickly moved from her wrist to clamp around her neck. "Just the same, I think I'll use you as my little insurance policy in case anyone tries to be a hero."

Rebecca felt a shudder of terror course through her as the man tightened his grip. He dragged her backward until her body was pressed against his chest while the gun stayed fixed on her forehead. The man sneered at the crowd, "Anybody moves and she's dead."

Peter felt himself go cold. He had to do something fast, but what? He saw the eyes of two of the tellers who shared a knowing look before one subtly reached below the counter. In that moment, Peter realized they had triggered the silent alarm!

The gunman turned back to the nearest teller. "What in the hell are you waiting for? Put the money in the fucking bag!

Now!"

Her movements were slow and deliberate when the teller started stuffing the bag with cash. *She's trying to stall to give the police time to arrive,* Peter thought.

"Don't you understand the words 'hurry up'?" the man shouted impatiently.

The guy paused, just long enough to shoot the next teller in the head. Her face was still in shock when a hot red spray burst from her forehead and spattered on Rebecca's cheek. He put the barrel back to Rebecca's temple, his eyes full of lunacy and rage.

"Now that you see how serious I am, how about we speed this up so no one else gets hurt?"

The man whispered into Rebecca's ear, "Except for you, sweet thing." He opened his mouth and ran his wet and slimy tongue along the side of her face. "Maybe I'll just take you with me so we can have a little fun together."

With trembling hands and quivering lips, the remaining teller filled the bag, daring to glimpse her fallen associate lying next to her, and handed it back to the man. He snatched it eagerly, pointing the gun at her for a moment with a twinkle in his eye and an evil grin across his lips.

The girl stood there shuddering in fear as she faced the specter of death that would have her join her fellow worker in the afterlife. She dared to breathe a small sigh of relief when the man pulled the gun away and backed up toward the foyer.

***

"You've got guts, sport, I'll give you that! Literally," Nybbas said. "I especially liked the wet, sucking sound your body made while you were rummaging around in your insides with your fingers. And then, when you dropped the key on the floor with only a few seconds to go...the drama was priceless! I couldn't have scripted it any better."

Michael heard the screams, followed by a gunshot a moment later, and he knew before it even registered where they were, that another innocent soul had been added to the body count.

They were standing in the foyer of a bank, just inside the entrance door, and Michael watched nervously as a lone gunman threatened the small crowd of customers, waving a gun around while he held tight to a female hostage. Then he saw Peter lying face down on the floor and gasped.

Nybbas said, "Yep, that's right. Your boy, Peter, is in another pickle. This time, though, you won't be able to save him. Instead, you'll be the one pulling the trigger."

Just like when Belial had pushed Michael's consciousness into Freddy, Nybbas compelled him forward until he merged with the gunman. Instantly, he was overwhelmed. He saw the past atrocities the criminal had committed—murder, rape, arson, theft—and knew this was a man Hell would welcome with open arms. Hatred. Anger. Rage. Bitterness. They all cut into Michael deeper than any blade could.

Nybbas was sitting beside him in a chair with a megaphone in his hand like a director on a movie set. "Now, I want you to pour everything you've got into this role. Find your inner madman and embrace it. Feel the desperation pouring through this doomed soul, something you can surely identify with, and let it all go. You are lost. There is no hope."

He paused for a second and then said, "Action!"

***

Peter saw a bright light materialize above Rebecca's head.

Images and visions of her and her family appeared to him in vivid detail. He saw her playing with her children; cuddling next to her husband; singing like an angel in the church choir.

He knew immediately what he needed to do. In that instant, everything made perfect sense. All the pieces of the puzzle came together perfectly. The scripture came into his mind instantly, *The Lord is my shepherd; I shall not want.*

Slowly, Peter rose. *He maketh me to lie down in green pastures: he leadeth me beside the still waters.*

He spoke as he rose, his voice loud and filled with confidence. "Let her go! Take me instead."

He restoreth my soul: he leadeth me in the paths of righteousness for his name's sake.

No, Peter! Please, don't do this! Michael begged silently.

The killer sized Peter up and sneered, "Why the fuck would I want you? You're not exactly my type. I think I'll stick with the lady here."

Peter stood firm. *Yea, though I walk through the valley of the shadow of death, I will fear no evil: for thou art with me; thy rod and thy staff, they comfort me.*

The distraction was just enough to allow two police officers to enter the building. "Freeze!" they shouted in unison as they locked their guns on him.

Peter took a step forward. *Thou preparest a table before me in the presence of mine enemies: thou anointest my head with oil; my cup runneth over.*

The man pushed the tip of the gun hard into Rebecca's temple. "Let me go or I swear I'll put a bullet through this lady's fucking skull!"

Another step forward. *Surely goodness and mercy shall follow me all the days of my life: and I will dwell in the house of the Lord forever.*

While the gunman was distracted, Peter rushed forward.

At the same time, Michael fought desperately to gain control, hoping to give Peter a chance to survive. But his endless battles against the darkness had left him powerless to stop the man's actions. That was if he had ever been strong enough to begin with?

The sorrow that enveloped Michael as he felt the man pull the gun from Rebecca's head and point it toward Peter was deeper than any he had felt before. He was powerless to stop the madness, and because of his weakness, a good man was going to die. Then, against his will, he felt the muscles inside the man's hand tighten as he pulled the trigger. *I'm sorry, Peter*, he thought, hoping his repentance would erase the sorrow he felt for the man he had just killed.

No, Peter, no! he cried as the bullet found its mark and hit Peter in the chest.

Peter's momentum carried him forward until he came crashing into the gunman, and Rebecca was sent sprawling to the floor, free of the present danger.

Tears filled his eyes as he felt his consciousness faltering. The pain in his chest became unbearable, but before he would succumb to the darkness, he had to make sure Rebecca was safe.

He turned his head to the side and saw the gunman climb back to his feet, only to be riddled with bullets and fall to the floor dead a second later.

Rebecca kneeled beside him, tears flowing like a raging river. Peter found the strength to raise his hand enough to grab hers, squeezing it tightly for a moment before he gave in to the darkness.

Chapter 15

Nybbas crouched down in front of Michael, who lay on the ground in a stupor. A pool of bile and mucus covered the dirt floor surrounding his face. "You know there's no chance for you to survive this, right?"

Michael responded with a slow wheeze as he struggled to breathe.

Nybbas chuckled, "Time for round three then, sport. That's if you're up for it?"

Abaddon purred softly as Nybbas rubbed her head. "I think this one's about done, my friend," Nybbas said. "One more shot should do it."

Abaddon responded with a soft meow before opening her mouth once more.

***

The heavily used work truck pulled into the parking lot of Dave's Place, a small diner on the outskirts of town. A minute later, Lucas got out of the truck and took a deep breath. He smiled wide as he walked his large and hungry frame toward the building.

Scott Dokey

The place was bustling with customers as Lucas entered and was immediately greeted by Patsy, a petite bubbly twenty-year-old girl with a bright smile.

"Hey, Lucas," Patsy said when he walked up to the hostess station. "How's it going?"

"Better now after seeing that smile of yours," Lucas replied, causing Patsy to blush.

He looked around at the crowded diner. "The place is hopping right now."

"Yeah, Rufus just put some new specials on the menu. You know how fast word travels around here."

"Well, you gotta give it to Rufus. His food is the best down-home cooking in the city."

"There's a table open in the corner, if that's good with you?"

"Yeah, that's fine."

Patsy led him through the dining area to a small table and placed a menu down in front of him.. "Sam will be with you shortly."

"Thank you," Lucas said as he sat down.

Almost immediately, Samantha, a pretty girl in her twenties, walked up. "Hey, Lucas," she said. "It's been a few weeks."

"Yeah, work's been crazy."

"I've missed that handsome smile around here."

Lucas chuckled. "Cool your jets, Sam. We're on the same team, remember?"

Samantha grinned. "Well, if you ever decide to switch sides, you know where to find me. In the meantime, you want your usual?"

"You know me so well!"

"See, we have this connection. I'm just saying..."

After Samantha walked away, a voice spoke up beside

him, "She's a cutie! I certainly wouldn't kick her out of bed for eating crackers."

Lucas looked at the table next to him and saw Nybbas sitting there dressed in a flannel shirt and cowboy hat. "Excuse me?" he said.

Nybbas replied, "I overheard your conversation and, man, she was all over you!"

"Then you also heard she's not my type."

"Sucks for you! If I was you, I'd think about changing things up for a minute just to tap that while you still got a chance."

"Well, you're not me, pal, so why don't you mind your own business?"

Nybbas held his arms up. "Okay, I get it. I'm just saying you should take advantage of every opportunity. You never know when your flame's gonna get snuffed out."

Lucas frowned at Nybbas, and then was interrupted as Samantha put a plate down on the table in front of him.

Nybbas got up from his table. "Enjoy your meal, boy. It just might be your last."

Lucas shot Nybbas an irritated look as he watched him walk toward the door. He shook his head, then focused on the plate in front of him for a second.

He'd been looking forward to this all day—a meal reminiscent of the dinners he and his family used to have every Sunday when they got together at Grandma's house so very long ago. Whether it was meatloaf and homemade mashed potatoes, or deep-fried chicken and corn on the cob, the food was always so good that you couldn't stop eating until you found yourself in a food coma. That's what Lucas was hoping for today—something that would remind him of Grandma.

She'd been dead for five years now, cancer claiming her life at the young age of eighty-eight—yet not a day went by where Lucas didn't think about her. For a long time, he'd been lost without her. After the tragedy of his parent's death when he was a teenager, she became the only family that he knew. A tear streamed down his face for a brief second before he brushed it away.

Sometimes he felt her nearby, and he knew she was watching over him. Today, as he was working on the assembly line, a smell somehow found its way through the dust and smoke, wafting its way to his nose. It was a smell that instantly told him she was there—the same smell that issued from the plate on the table before him now—country-fried steak smothered in rich, creamy pepper gravy, a large helping of mashed potatoes, and sweet rolls; Grandma's favorite meal. It was just like home. Almost.

Lucas dug in eagerly, almost desperate even, to reclaim something that he'd lost. No sooner had he gotten the first bite into his mouth when the room spun rapidly. His eyes blurred, and he felt dizzy. He braced himself in his chair to steady himself.

Samantha rushed over with a worried look on her face. "Lucas? Are you alright?"

Lucas stuttered as he spoke, "I'll...I'll be okay. Just a little dizzy, that's all."

She smiled at him. "How about a glass of water?"

He nodded in response and leaned back in his chair.

As soon as Samantha left, flames shot up from the middle of the table. Lucas jumped back and nearly fell to the floor. Then an image appeared in the flames: a woman standing outside screaming frantically while her house was on fire. She clutched an infant to her chest while she cried out for her other child.

Lucas recognized the woman immediately. It was

Gretchen, his next-door neighbor, and the little boy she called desperately for was her four-year-old son, Justin. The vision shifted and Lucas was now standing in the attic of the two-story house, watching Justin scream for help, his face covered in soot. Then the image was gone. The vision was over.

Lucas jumped from his chair, threw a $20 bill on the table, and rushed out of the restaurant. His home-cooked meal and the trip down memory lane would have to wait for another day.

"I'm sure glad I didn't have what he had!" Nybbas said with a chuckle as Lucas raced past him.

As he ran toward his car, Lucas scanned the afternoon sky, searching for signs of a catastrophe. For a second, he thought he saw a wisp of smoke drifting through the air.

The very forces of nature seemed against him as he raced home. Every streetlight he approached turned red and stayed that way a lot longer than normal. At least half a dozen animals wandered precariously onto the road, tempting fate and forcing Lucas to slam on the brakes. Finally, when he was only three blocks from home, a train decided Lucas hadn't been delayed enough yet and began a slow crawl along the tracks.

That's when Lucas saw it—a huge, black cloud of smoke rising into the air just ahead of him, threatening to choke out the sun. His heart sank. The train lurched and then came to a complete stop for a second before inching its way forward once more.

Finally, the last car passed in front of him and he flew around the crossing guards. A minute later, he came to a screeching halt in front of his neighbor's house and jumped out of the car.

For a second, Lucas stood there stunned. Everything was exactly as he had seen in the vision at the restaurant.

Gretchen rushed over, crying hysterically, "Lucas, you've got to help me! Justin's still in there!"

He tried to calm her down. "Don't worry, Gretchen. I'll get Justin out. I promise."

Inside, Lucas hoped he could live up to that promise.

Chapter 16

Michael stood outside the house as Lucas rushed up the steps toward disaster. Suddenly, the man stopped, frozen in time and space.

Without turning around, he knew Nybbas was there.

"You know he's not coming out of there alive," Nybbas said.

It's true, Michael thought as he watched the horror unfold. *No ordinary person could survive this.*

What Lucas saw as a devastating fire engulfing a building, Michael saw as a trio of fire demons laying waste to someone's life, ripping away everything they had worked for, everything that was dear to them, including their children.

"To show that I'm not all heartless," Nybbas continued, "I'm going to give you a chance to save him, Sport. If you succeed in saving the boy, then he'll live to be a ripe old man, enjoying tequila shots from the navel of some bimbo on the beach during the twilight of his life. If you don't, then you'll have more blood on your hands. It'll be one more life lost because of you."

Michael looked up at the inferno that surrounded the structure and knew it was a suicide mission. As if the demons scurrying about weren't enough, he watched in horror as a large behemoth erupted from the ground behind the building. As dark as ash, with fire pulsing through its veins, it resembled a living volcano as it moved. A long fiery whip hung at its side, its barbs setting the ground on fire as it walked toward the house.

"Agramon! You made it!" Nybbas said. "I wasn't sure if you were available."

The demon roared at Nybbas as he brought his whip down on the corner of the house, sending a large section of the structure crashing to the ground.

"As you can see, the situation just got a little more intense," Nybbas said.

"How am I supposed to beat that?" Michael asked in disbelief.

Nybbas shrugged, "Not my problem. I guess you'll have to figure it out? Remember, save the boy and Lucas lives. If not, oh well."

Nybbas disappeared, leaving Michael staring in fear at the colossal beast as it approached. *What am I supposed to do here? That thing's gonna destroy me in a second.*

Then he remembered Nybbas' instructions—save the boy and Lucas lives. He didn't need to defeat the demon. He just needed to rescue the boy! He looked at the burning house and his heart sank again. The boy was trapped in an inferno at the highest part of the house, surrounded by demons. His only chance was to try to dodge the demon attacks and run through the blaze as fast as he could toward the attic. With a little bit of luck, he just might make it. *Who am I kidding? It's going to take a fucking miracle!*

But he had to try. Someone's life was on the line. Again.

Michael drew a deep breath and then raced up the stairs, lowering his shoulder as he ran. The door gave way under the impact and flew open. Immediately, he was hit with an unbearable wave of searing pain as the fire eagerly engulfed him.

He felt the skin on his face and hands start to melt under the intense heat while his eyes stung from the smoke. His lungs became constricted with each passing second, choking off his oxygen, but he had to go on. He pushed himself forward desperately toward the staircase leading to the second floor. *I just need to rescue the boy!*

The house trembled as Agramon brought his whip down again, this time dangerously close to Michael, and he staggered sideways to avoid the blow. Meanwhile, one of the fire demons had closed in on him from behind. He cried out as it clamped one of its fiery claws around his ankle and yanked him to the floor.

Michael rolled onto his back as the demon leaped toward him. Desperately, he reached out for anything he could grab onto. His fingers wrapped around a burning timber that had splintered off, and just as the demon was about to land on him, he impaled the thing through the chest. A sharp shrill echoed through the burning structure for a moment before it died.

He hardly had time to recover before the second one sent a fireball racing toward him. Quickly, Michael rolled to his right, avoiding the main impact of the deadly missile, but the heat from the attack was unbearable. As his skin began to blister and boil, he knew he wouldn't last much longer.

Desperately, he crawled toward the stairs and willed himself up. Each step was met with incredible pain as he ascended toward the second floor, using the banister as a crutch to pull him forward. The skin on his hands had become black and charred, leaving behind hand-prints of ash. Up above, he heard the young boy crying desperately for help.

Michael was almost to the top when Agramon's whip came crashing down right in front of him, splitting the staircase in two. With a bone-crushing thud, he hit the floor a second later and watched helplessly as the towering demon brought his foot down hard on his chest, crushing him.

Nybbas appeared a second later, kneeling beside Michael's broken body. "So, so close! You actually had me thinking you might make it there for a minute. Now you get to watch another person die because of you!"

A weak groan ushered from Michael's mouth before everything went dark.

***

Lucas saw tentacles of flame dancing in the living room through the large picture window as he raced onto the front porch. He reached the top step just as the window exploded, sending shards of glass lurching through the air like missiles. The force of the blow sent Lucas sprawling onto the deck.

He staggered back to his feet, his face bleeding from several cuts where the glass had ripped open his skin. He charged the front door, ramming it hard with his shoulder and wincing in pain at the impact. Luckily, the heat from the fire had weakened the surrounding frame, and the door flew open with a crash.

Flames completely engulfed the living room to his right, with the dining room opposite, destined to become the next casualty. His target, though, was the staircase and its impenetrable wall of flames straight ahead.

Frantically, he looked around for anything he might use as a shield that would enable him to leap through the deadly barrier. Lucas thought he could hear Justin's muffled cries overhead. Desperation became the driving force as he rushed toward the steps, prepared to endure any physical blow the fire might deliver.

Suddenly, the flames in front of him disappeared. Lucas stood at the foot of the stairs for a brief second in total shock. Then he bound up the stairs to the second floor. When he reached the top step, he was startled to find himself face to face with his grandma. He knew immediately that it was she who had cleared the flames for him.

His lips trembled as he spoke, "Grandma? Is that really you?"

Lucas felt a tug on his heart as tears blurred his vision. His grandma put her finger to her mouth to quiet his soul before turning and walking down the hallway. She then disappeared through the second door on the left.

***

"That's not in the script!" Nybbas yelled.

Gabriel appeared a second later from the water, dragging a long and lifeless tentacle behind him. "I thought it could use a little re-write," he said.

Nybbas turned toward Gabriel with a scowl on his face. "What in the fuck are you doing here, Gabriel?"

Gabriel replied, "I think you know why I'm here, Nybbas."

Nybbas turned to Abaddon, "Watch over our friend here while I take care of our intruder." A large sword materialized in his hand.

"You know you can't win this war," Gabriel said.

"Belial seems to think so. For me, that's good enough."

"You always were a fool, Nybbas, following those who would steer you down the wrong path."

"Let's see who's the fool when I slice you in half and feed

your insides to Abaddon."

Nybbas swung his sword around, but Gabriel quickly blocked the attack with a sword of his own.

"Are you sure you want to do this, Nybbas?" Gabriel said.

The only answer the demon gave was a loud roar, followed by a flurry of attacks.

***

Lucas sprinted to the door and lunged for the handle, feeling a searing pain rush through him as his skin met with the scorching metal. He hissed in agony and settled his blistered palm against his chest, watching as it smoked from the burn.

Desperately, he kicked at the door and it splintered open, revealing an opposite door that stood ajar. With a roar of determination, Lucas raced over, hearing Justin's cries become louder with each step he took. His heart raced as he scrambled up the stairs, only to stumble when a beam suddenly plummeted down towards him. He threw himself to the side, feeling a sharp snap in his leg as his knee collided with the edge of the steps. Fireworks of pain burst across his vision as he rolled away, screaming in agony, knowing that both of their lives were suddenly in danger.

Another scream from Justin jolted Lucas back to his senses. Adrenaline and desperation gave him the strength to continue. He called out to the boy, "Justin, it's me, Lucas, your next-door neighbor. Don't worry, kiddo, we're gonna get you out of here, okay?"

"I'm scared, Lucas," Justin cried out.

"I know. Me too. But we're gonna get out of here. I promise. Right now, I need your help. Can you make it to the stairs?"

Another explosion caused the entire house to shake. Lucas

heard Justin cry out once more.

"Justin, we're running out of time. Can you make it to the stairs?"

There was no answer.

Then, a moment later, Lucas was looking up at a soot-covered face that partially resembled the little boy he had seen playing outside countless times before. His blond hair was matted with dirt, and he had a long cut across his cheek.

"I need you to climb onto my back. Can you do that? I'm gonna give you a piggyback ride out of here. How's that sound?"

Justin didn't answer, but did as he was told and fastened himself securely around Lucas' waist and neck. Then Lucas limped gingerly down the stairs back to Justin's room.

A blanket lay draped over the end of the bed, untouched by the ravaging fire, and Lucas was sure that it hadn't been there a moment before. A gift from his grandma, he was sure.

He flipped the blanket back over his head so that Justin was completely covered. He tried to cover his own mouth with it as well, but it was too short. Instead, he grabbed the corners tight with both hands and pulled them as low as possible to ensure that the deadly smoke wouldn't find its way into Justin's lungs.

Lucas limped as quickly as possible out of the room and back down the hall toward the stairs. Each step sent a jolt of excruciating pain through Lucas' body, but he had to go on. He knew that his soul would never be at peace if he failed to save this boy.

Again, he was met with a wall of flames at the top of the stairs, and once more, an unseen force vanquished the flames. He looked down and saw his grandma smiling up at him in approval. She turned and walked to the front door, parting the sea of flames for them as she went.

Feebly, Lucas hobbled down the stairs and nearly fell before reaching the bottom. He limped toward the front door and saw firefighters rushing into the blaze. A deep feeling of relief surged through him as they pulled Justin from his shoulders and took him to safety.

Lucas vaguely felt himself being picked up and carried out of the house to a gurney at the edge of the lawn. He turned his head and saw Gretchen crying uncontrollably while she held tight to her son.

Then he saw his grandma standing behind Gretchen, smiling. She walked over to Lucas with pride beaming on her face and reached out to him.

"Come with me, Lucas. There's something special waiting for you."

He reached his hand toward hers, and she helped him to his feet.

"But Grandma, I don't understand?"

"Don't worry, dear. You will."

As they walked away from the smoldering house, Lucas looked back and saw his burned and broken body still lying on the gurney. He looked at his grandma and saw the perfect expression of love on her face.

Then he understood completely.

***

Michael was dimly aware of the crackle of the timbers as the flames continued their attack on the house. He smelled the thick smoke that hung in the air, heard the woman's desperate cries, and knew he was still trapped in the same nightmare.

When he opened his eyes, he saw Lucas lying unmoving on the gurney, and his heart sank. He had failed again and his soul crumbled a little more under the weight of another death he could've prevented.

Suddenly, he felt the familiar searing pain in his skull again, and his vision grew blurry. But just before everything went black, he saw something that shocked him. The spirit of the brave man who had given his life to save the boy rose from his body and walked away, being led away by an older woman with the knowledge and kindness in her eyes that only a grandmother could possess.

The woman turned and looked directly at Michael with a smile on her face and winked. For a brief second, an instant almost undetectable, he saw Gabriel looking back at him.

Chapter 17

Nybbas walked back to join Abaddon next to Michael. His suit was slashed in numerous places so that one sleeve was barely hanging on by a thread, he had a long cut across one cheek, and a section of his hair had been chopped off.

"Now, where were we before we were so rudely interrupted?" he said. "Ah, yes, Michael. How are you doing in there, Sport?"

He crouched down and looked closely at Michael, smiling at the puddle of drool that had formed under his chin as he lay on the cave floor.

He stood up and spread his arms out wide like a theater company director announcing the opening of a long-anticipated stage-play, "Now, for the fourth and final act, I give you 'Dead Beat Dad with Anger Management Issues!'"

Abaddon tilted her head to one side and meowed.

"What? Too long?" Nybbas asked. He thought for a second, "You're right. How about 'Bad Blood'? Or 'Deadly Wrath'? Or wait, I know, 'Another One Bites the Dust?'"

Abaddon meowed again, questioningly.

"Hey, it's one of my favorite songs," Nybbas said. "Anyway, you know what to do."

***

A soft snore escaped John's lips as he lay stretched out in his green scrubs on the couch in the corner the hospital lounge. A dark shadow passed through the room unseen a moment before the alarm on his phone went off, jolting him awake.

After silencing his phone, he sat up groggily and rubbed his eyes to pry the sleep from them. A wide yawn, followed by a long stretch brought him awake enough to quickly down an energy drink so he could continue his double shift. *Ah, the life of an RN,* he thought dourly.

John walked down the hallway, past one of the emergency suites with the curtain open, and stopped when he saw a young woman with her back toward him and her head bent low.

He immediately recognized her as his neighbor and rushed over to her. "Erica? Are you okay? What's wrong?"

When the woman turned around to look at him with a blank, haunted stare, John stopped. "Sorry. I thought you were someone else."

John quickly backed away and continued down the hall. Cold sweat quickly gathered on his brow, and a shiver ran through his spine when he found an identical woman sitting in every suite, each one wearing the same clothes, and each one with the same haunted look on her face.

His pace quickened until he pushed desperately through the double doors that exited the emergency area. Once he had put a little distance between himself and the horrific ensemble of doppelgangers, he stopped and leaned against the wall, shaking. "Oh my God, what the fuck was that?" he exclaimed as he tried to shake the image of the women from his brain.

John took a few deep breaths to calm himself before pulling a bottle of pills from his pocket and popping a couple in his mouth, swallowing hard. "Man, these long shifts are finally getting to me!" he said as he tried to calm himself down. "Might be time to take a few days off?"

Suddenly, he doubled over in pain and cried out as he dropped to his knees. "Holy shit!"

After a few minutes of writhing in agony, John stumbled to his feet and shuffled down the hall toward the bathroom door. After darting inside, he rushed into the nearest stall, where he wretched violently.

A minute later, he exited the stall and bent over the nearest sink to splash cold water on his face. As he wiped his face off, Nybbas strolled in wearing a doctor's coat and stopped at one of the urinals to relieve himself.

"You okay there, Sport?" Nybbas asked.

John nodded at him weakly. "Yeah. I think it's just something I ate that didn't agree with me."

"Well, I hope for your sake that's all it is. Lots of crazy things going around right now."

After washing his hands under the faucet next to John, Nybbas dried them off and tossed the crinkled paper towel into the trash before he turned and left, whistling buoyantly. As John followed him out the door, he didn't notice that Nybbas' reflection in the mirror was still standing there smirking at him.

John shambled up to the nurse's station, where the Head Nurse, Nancy, a grumpy woman in her fifties, sat at her computer with a dour look on her face. "Hey, Nancy," he said weakly. "I'm not feeling too well. If it's okay with you, I'm gonna call it a day."

Nancy lowered her glasses and glared at him. "It most certainly is not okay with me. We're swamped and already short-staffed as it is. I need you to suck it up and finish your shift."

John was about to say something, when Nybbas walked up.

"I wouldn't be too hard on the kid," Nybbas said. "I was there after he puked his guts out a few minutes ago. And let me tell you, it wasn't pretty."

"And you are?" Nancy asked.

Nybbas extended his hand to Nancy. "Sorry. I'm Dr. Smith. I just transferred from Mercy General."

Nancy's brow wrinkled. "I don't recall hearing about any transfer?"

Nybbas chuckled. "Just kind of happened spur of the moment. I'm sure word will get out soon."

Nybbas pats John on the shoulder. "It was a pleasure to meet you, John. I certainly hope you feel better soon."

As soon as Nybbas' hand touches him, John's stomach gurgled loudly again, and he reached desperately for a trash can nearby, grabbing it just in time.

"I guess that's a no about feeling better?" Nybbas said.

Nancy glanced at Nybbas questioningly and then turned to John. "Okay, fine. Get out of here before I change my mind."

Nybbas chuckled as he watched Nancy cringe as she looked at the trash can in disgust, while John lumbered down the hall.

"This oughta be fun!" Nybbas said as he walked away.

***

A chorus of yells and jeers rang through Michael's ears,

forcing him to open his eyes. When he did, he was shocked to find that he was trapped inside a large octagon-shaped cage. The walls extended ten feet high on all sides, with a chain-link roof enclosing the top. Blood stained the canvas floor of the arena, while an enormous pile of what looked like ripped out flesh lay just a few feet to his right. A swarm of flies fed hungrily on whatever remains they were.

He looked around for an escape, but saw none. What he did see was a large and bald Hispanic man standing across from him shirtless, his hands wrapped tightly with white tape. His body was covered in tattoos and he wore the face of a hardened criminal.

The crowd that cried and cheered at the sight of the big man was made up of twisted and disfigured creatures that yelled and spit at Michael from the other side of the cage. The thick smell of sulfur told him that he was in Hell once more. The hatred pouring out of the man across from told him he was going to have to fight for his life. Again.

Their howls erupted further when Nybbas' voice broke through the throng from a speaker overhead. "Ladies and gentlemen—and I use those terms loosely—for tonight's main attraction, in the far corner, I give you Clyde. Some call him a dead-beat. Some call him a wife-beater. I just call him mis-understood."

The crowd cheered and howled as Clyde stepped toward the center of the ring, his eyes cold as steel.

Then Nybbas' voice rang through again, "And in the near corner, I present Michael. Well...judge for yourself. He's a miserable excuse for a human if there ever was one."

The crowd booed and jeered, while Michael stood silently in shock. *This guy's as big as a fucking tank!*

"Now, the rules of the fight are simple," Nybbas said. "Basically, there are no rules. Anything goes. Sudden death.

If you win, Michael, then everything goes away and you return to your pitiful life, never to be bothered again. If you lose, an eternity in Hell will be waiting for you with open arms."

Like the announcer at a boxing match, Nybbas cried loudly, "Let's get ready to rumble!"

The crowd roared and cheered as the bell sounded and Clyde advanced toward Michael, his fists closed tightly, his eyes cold and dark.

As soon as Clyde was within striking distance, he threw a wide right hook that barely missed Michael's jaw as he staggered backward. The follow-through caused Clyde to stumble forward and gave Michael a chance to throw a punch of his own. Not really much of a fighter, he pulled his arm back and punched as hard as he could, hoping more than anything else just to connect. The shot to Clyde's stomach found the mark, but he might as well have punched a bean bag. The blow had absolutely no effect.

A wicked sneer crossed Clyde's lips for a brief second as Michael stood there stunned. Before Michael could react, Clyde reached out with his left hand and grabbed Michael by the throat with a grip as strong as a vise.

Michael gasped for air as he felt his windpipe strain under the attack and feebly tried to pull the man's hand away. Finally, in a last-ditch effort to free himself, he brought his foot up and kicked Clyde hard in the crotch.

The effort proved successful, as Clyde immediately released his hold on Michael and fell to his knees, howling in pain.

Michael immediately dropped to the floor, choking and wheezing as his lungs cried for oxygen, but even as he felt air rushing back in, allowing him to breathe again, Clyde was already recovering from his attack.

As he staggered to his feet, Clyde closed in on him once again. Michael tried to dodge the next punch, but he was too weak, and this time the punch connected squarely on Michael's jaw, sending him spinning. As soon as he was on the floor, Clyde pounced on him, straddling his chest, and devastated him with a flurry of punches.

Teetering on the verge of unconsciousness, with his eyes blurry from blood and tears, Michael glanced at the cheering crowd, which yelled and howled their approval at his quick demise. *I guess they're getting what they paid for?* He thought bitterly.

Then he saw, for a brief second once more, Gabriel sitting in the front row watching the fight with a warm smile on his face. He nodded briefly at Michael before he disappeared. One word echoed through Michael's mind. *Surrender.*

His mind flashed quickly through all the torture that Nybbas had put him through, and he realized there was one particular recurring theme—the sacrifice of one life to save another. Ruth, Peter, Lucas, they had all given their lives to save someone else. And in each case, Nybbas had tried to get Michael to stop the scenario from unfolding before that could happen. *I know what your game is, demon!*

Michael closed his eyes and calmed his mind. "I surrender," he whispered.

Chapter 18

John stared at himself in the mirror, his face a tortured reflection of the hours he had spent in the hospital and the sudden onset of the mysterious illness that had left him weak and spent. His red-rimmed eyes were sunken deep in their sockets like two moons at midnight, and his ink-black hair was an unruly mop atop his head. He smelled the rank funk coming off him in waves, along with a lingering queasiness that still twisted his gut. He lifted his arm and took a whiff. "Yeah, that's ripe!"

Despite the long days and tough cases, he was grateful for his job. It brought him a sense of belonging that he had never experienced before, especially after all the mistakes he had made growing up. It felt right to be in a place to help others cope with their struggles, even if it reminded him of his own painful past.

He pressed his hand against the wall switch and listened as the rickety fan sputtered to life, followed by an ear-splitting thud before it went completely quiet. He looked up at the ceiling with a frown.

With weariness weighing heavy on him, he turned on the shower and peeled off his scrubs. He stepped under the hot spray and stood there motionless until slivers of energy slowly returned to life inside his veins. A little more alive than before, he cleaned the dirt and grime from his body before switching off the water and stepping out.

As the steam from his shower slowly cleared, he stepped closer to the mirror and wiped away the fog so he could get a better look. His breath caught in his throat when he ran the brush through his hair and saw that a chunk had come out with it.

"No way, I'm too young for this!" he exclaimed, half in frustration and half in denial. With a despairing sigh, he hastily tried to cover the patch with the long strands from the other side, only to find that they were nowhere near enough. Knowing that it would be futile, yet clinging to a flicker of hope, he brushed through his hair again and stared at his reflection.

A loud shattering sound echoed from John's bedroom and he quickly spun around, nearly stumbling over himself in surprise as he stopped in the doorway and looked toward the window. Pulling the blinds up, he gasped as he saw a small crack spider webbing its way across the glass, and the light of an overhead street lamp revealed a pair of dead black birds lying motionless on the alley floor three stories below. His heart raced as two more black birds flew into the glass, their tiny bodies bouncing off the window pane before they fell motionless to join the others. He shuddered at the eerie silence that ensued after the birds' final quivers had passed.

With a concerned look in his eyes, he threw on a pair of sweatpants and a T-shirt before he left the bedroom, feeling the same dread from before creeping back in.

John's eyes widened in shock as he walked into the living room and found Erica standing in the doorway, her posture slumped and shoulders shaking. He moved closer and noticed a deep purple bruise around her left eye, the skin broken near her cut lip, and his heart sank at the sight of her right arm held so tightly to her stomach that eh feared it was broken.

He glanced out at the hallway before gently closing the door behind them. Rage boiled up inside him; this was all too familiar. Silently, he cursed the man across the hall; damned him to an eternity of torment.

"I'm so scared, John," Erica sobbed. "He's gotten out of control. I'm afraid he won't stop this time until I'm dead." Her eyes trembled with fear, and her breathing came in gasps as she struggled to reign in her terror. "What am I going to do?"

John tried his best to calm her down. "Shh, it'll be alright. The first thing we need to do is call the police. They'll be able to handle Clyde and keep you safe. Then we need to get you to the hospital immediately."

Then a horrible thought entered his head: Destiny wasn't with Erica! She was alone in the apartment with that madman! He said quickly, "We have to get your daughter—"

"Don't worry," Erica interrupted. "She's spending the night at my mother's. That's what started the whole thing tonight. Clyde thought the whole reason for her to stay at my mom's was so I could cheat on him. No matter how much I insist that I've never been unfaithful, he still believes that I have." She started crying again. "Why won't he believe me?"

"Some people only believe what they want to believe; see what they want to see."

She sighed tiredly, "He wasn't always like that."

"I know."

"There was a time when he was happy; when he was fun to be around. I don't know...Maybe it's my fault somehow?"

"Don't be ridiculous. None of this your fault."

The door suddenly burst open and Clyde rushed into the room. He was a large man, tall and round, with a bald head and goatee. And his face was full of rage. "I should've known I'd find you here, you fucking slut."

"It's not like that, Clyde, and you know it!" John said as the man stood there like a volcano ready to erupt.

"Shut up, asshole, or you'll get the same thing she got," Clyde replied.

Erica pleaded with him, "Please don't hurt him, Clyde. He didn't do anything."

"Shut up, you filthy whore!" Clyde yelled before slapping her hard across the face and sending her tumbling to the floor, where she landed with a howl on her broken arm.

John was just about to move in on him when Clyde pulled a knife out of his back pocket. The blade sprung out with a click and immediately he grabbed Erica and pulled her up to him, yanking her roughly by the hair.

He brandished the blade of the weapon against her throat, "Don't try anything stupid, mother-fucker."

***

"You had a chance to stop this and you failed once again," Nybbas said.

Michael looked at the man who had just annihilated him quickly and easily, and then he looked at John, an innocent man with a purpose in life. For a second, he felt sad. That sadness turned to anger when he thought about all the needless deaths that had happened recently. Lives lost that shouldn't have. "I know what you're trying to do and it won't work."

Nybbas looked at Michael and laughed. "We'll see about that! Don't even try to pretend that you know me, boy!"

***

Just then, the window behind Clyde lit up like a blazing sun. Intoxicating music swirled in John's ears and he heard angelic voices singing, enveloping him in an indescribable warmth. He felt his heart expand with a joyous sensation beyond anything he had ever experienced before.

Then the window went blank again, showing only the cold and dismal alleyway below it. It was clear that no one else but him had seen the light, heard the voices, or felt the love - but he understood what had to be done.

"Come on," John shouted, "quit hiding behind the woman and face me like a man!"

Clyde responded with a sneer, "No way, man! You think I'm stupid?"

"No. Just a coward. Only a coward would hide behind a defenseless woman with a broken arm."

This last bit did just the trick. The worst thing you can ever call a bully is a coward, and the man standing before him was the biggest bully John had ever seen.

Clyde threw Erica to the side like a discarded toy. A loud cry flew from her mouth as her head struck the corner of the coffee table before hitting the floor. For an instant, John feared the blow had killed her, but then she rolled over slowly, indicating she was alive at least.

As soon as she was out of the way, John lunged at Clyde with all the ferocity of a jungle cat pouncing on its prey. He felt the knife blade penetrate deeply into his abdomen as he grappled with the man; felt the warm liquid oozing out of his body; felt the imminent presence of Death standing nearby.

But he was determined that Death would not have him until he had rid the world of this horrible man. He grabbed Clyde tightly with both hands in a mighty bear hug and then hurled the two of them with all his might toward the window. The glass shattered as the mass of bodies flew toward the open space beyond.

John glimpsed Clyde's face, which was full of surprise, as they fell toward the alleyway below. His expression gave John a bit of vindication before they both hit the ground with a bone-shattering impact and died.

As his spirit rose through the air, John glanced down and saw Clyde's soul being dragged toward the inferno that waited for him eagerly. He also saw a physically and emotionally broken young lady lying on his apartment floor. But now, she and her daughter were free from the torment they had endured far too long. They could finally live the life they deserved.

Chapter 19

Nybbas walked up to Michael's prone body and kicked him hard in the stomach. Even though his eyes were still milky and drool dribbled from the corner of his mouth, a soft moan escaped his lips from the impact. It was barely audible, and Nybbas was too caught up in his failure to hear it, but it was there.

"What the fuck just happened, Abaddon?!"

Abaddon responded with a questioning meow.

Before he could comment further, Gabriel walked up out of the water, this time empty-handed, but not without purpose. "Just like so many times in the past, Nybbas, you have underestimated the power of the human spirit."

"Don't give me that crap! You interfered, and you know it!"

"All I did was simply help him see things in a different light. He did the rest on his own."

"Bullshit! There's no way this pathetic excuse of a man was strong enough to beat me on his own."

"Once again, you fail to see things as they truly are," Gabriel said. "I suggest you look behind you."

Nybbas turned around and was shocked to see Michael

struggling to his feet. "That's impossible! His brain should be mush by now!" He turned back around and walked up to Gabriel, pointing his finger in the angel's chest, "How did you do this?"

"Nybbas!" Michael roared. "You're going to pay for all the shit you've caused!"

When Nybbas turned back around quickly, a look of panic was unfolding in his eyes. "Hey, I was just doing my job and following orders. Believe me, it was nothing personal."

"It felt kinda personal to me," Michael said.

The demon looked back and forth from Michael to Gabriel like a cornered rat. Finally, he scooped up Abaddon and said, "Come on, Abaddon. I think we're done here."

Then he and the feline vanished.

As soon as they were gone, Michael slumped to his knees, completely exhausted, both mentally and physically. His brain was still on fire from Abaddon's attack, and he felt like he had just been run over by a truck. Thinking back to Clyde's attack, he pretty much had.

Gabriel put his arm around Michael's shoulder and said, "I think it's time to get out of here."

Michael looked at him weakly, "Sounds good to me. I don't feel so good."

The two of them vanished for a second before reappearing in Michael's apartment.

Michael stumbled to the couch and flopped down. Gabriel placed his hand on Michael's forehead and closed his eyes for a moment, healing Michael from the effects of Abaddon's poisons.

"Thank you," Michael said weakly.

Gabriel replied, "No, thank you. You did this on your own. Your will is to be commended."

Michael slumped further into the couch. For a long time,

he just sat there, quiet and somber, trying to process everything he'd just gone through. After a while, he spoke up, "I don't understand what's going on? Why didn't Nybbas just kill me? Why all the games?"

"Nybbas wasn't trying to kill you, per se, although if you had died, I'm sure he wouldn't have minded. No, his job was to try to stop the other four from sacrificing themselves. And if he couldn't do that, then he would try to break your spirit so that you would give up."

"Couldn't he have just killed any of them, or even me, for that matter?"

"Death has rules that even demons must follow."

"But why them?" Michael asked.

Gabriel smiled. "We chose these four much in the same way Belial chose his four doomed souls. They will become the Four Chosen Ones who will battle Belial's Four Horsemen, and you, my dear Michael, are the one who's going to lead them."

Michael's jaw dropped. "What the fuck did you just say?"

Gabriel replied calmly, "It's quite simple, Michael. You're going to lead the Chosen Ones into battle and destroy Belial's army."

"That's easy for you to say. Look at me. I'm a fucking mess. I can't possibly lead anyone."

"That's not true, Michael. You're simply a tortured soul, hurting from an attack you were unprepared to fight. Just know that you are stronger than you believe. Trust me, I've been around for a long time. I know true power when I see it. You just have to see it in yourself."

Michael looked into Gabriel's eyes and saw the truth shining through. The images of the four who had unselfishly given their lives filled his head. Then he thought of his own life and how insignificant he had always felt. This was his chance to mean something.

As if Gabriel could sense another question about to issue from Michael's lips, he said, "For now, I suggest you get a good night's sleep, knowing the nightmares can no longer harm you. We'll talk more in the morning."

Gabriel disappeared, leaving Michael in quiet contemplation about the purpose of his life and the uncertain future he was facing. After a minute, he got up and shuffled out of the room.

***

The next morning, Michael woke with a start to find Gabriel sitting on the edge of his bed. "How long have you been there?" he asked.

Gabriel replied, "For a while. I was just making sure you were okay."

"Yeah, that's not creepy at all," Michael mumbled as he swung his legs out of bed and got up. "Before we talk, I need food. And coffee...lots and lots of coffee."

Michael was shocked to find a box of doughnuts and a fresh-brewed pot of coffee waiting for him in the kitchen. After pouring a cup, he devoured a doughnut in record time and grabbed another one before sitting down at the table.

"The sugar and caffeine should help recover fully from Abaddon's attack," Gabriel said.

"Speaking of which...what the hell was that thing?"

Gabriel replied, "Abaddon is an ancient demon of incredible power. How she came to be associated with Nybbas I have no idea. She's usually a little more discerning regarding the company she keeps."

"Yeah, that guy's a real dick!"

"That he is. But given his propensity for self-preservation, I don't imagine we'll be seeing him again anytime soon."

Michael finished his second doughnut and took a long sip of his coffee. "Okay, say I believe you about all of this apocalyptic shit and decide to play my part. What would I need to do?"

Gabriel's reply was simple: "First, you would need to die."

"I was afraid you were going to say something like that."

Michael sat there in deep thought for a long time. His mind was swimming in an ocean of confusion as he sorted through everything that had happened. All the torment, all the pain, all the suffering, it had all led him here. Accepting one's destiny is often not a simple thing, especially when the path chosen is completely out of your control. But eventually, a feeling of resignation comes over you, and you realize that the only course to follow is the one spread out before you. He laid back on the couch and closed his eyes, finally surrendering himself to his fate.

"What now?" he asked.

"You are free to do whatever you like for the next day and a half. Thursday evening, you are to go to St. Anthony's Cathedral, where all the preparations have been made. Father Thomas will be expecting you."

Suddenly Gabriel was gone, leaving him feeling more alone and afraid than ever. For a long time, all he could think was, *I'm going to die soon!* It didn't matter the reason, or that it was for a higher purpose. Those were still hard words to swallow. Plus, there were so many things he hadn't done in his life; so many hopes and dreams that he'd pissed away.

Michael's mind was a tangled mess of emotions as he made his way to the bathroom, where he splashed cold water on his face before looking in the mirror. He stared at himself for a long time, trying to convince himself that he was worthy. The needle marks in his arms said otherwise.

He fell to his knees and held his arms out, crying for the strength and courage to follow through. Praying for the first time since he could remember, the words just stumbled out of his mouth. "Oh, God, please give me the strength to go through with this!"

Finally, exhaustion set in and he fell asleep on the bathroom floor.

Chapter 20

As Michael trudged along the sidewalk the next morning, one thought repeated through his brain, over and over. He had fucked up, yet again. He needed to talk to Mary but didn't know what he was going to say, if she would even talk to him at all, that is. *She deserves better. Maybe when I'm gone, she can find that.* It was only now, in his last moments, that he realized how perfect his life would've been if he hadn't pushed her away.

When he reached the front door of the building, he pressed the button on the intercom. A few seconds later, Mary's voice crackled through the speaker, "Who is it?"

Michael hesitated for a second and pressed the button once more. "Mary, it's me."

Her response was expected. "What do you want?" she snapped.

"I'm sorry I ran out on you at the hospital. I just got really freaked out. Can I please come up? I need to talk to you."

The intercom was silent for a long time. Desperately, Michael pressed the button once more, "Please, Mary, it's important."

Finally, he heard the click that opened the main entrance

and a sigh of relief escaped his lips. He rushed up to the second floor and was just about to knock when the door opened to reveal Mary standing there waiting for him with a scorned look on her face.

"Well, what's so fucking important that you had to rush up here?" she sniped.

Michael cringed at the hurt in her voice. "I'm sorry, Mary. I didn't mean to hurt you."

Mary looked at Michael coldly through the open doorway. She loved the tortured man in front of her with all her heart, but she couldn't keep going this way. She knew he was using again. The signs were all there. But she also knew that something else was going on with him that went far beyond the drugs. She had even experienced a little bit of it too. He was hurting, but the fact that he kept shutting her out made her hurt just as bad.

"Who do you think you are, Michael, that you can come crawling back here time after time on your hands and knees and I'll forget everything? Every time I reach out to help you shut me out. How am I supposed to act?"

"But I don't mean to," Michael responded.

"You never mean to, Michael. That's just it! You never think before you act. I was scared to death at the hospital. I sat there and watched while your body jerked and twitched on the table. Nothing the doctor did could wake you. I was fucking terrified! Then, when you did finally wake up, you left me all alone. No words to let me know you were okay. Nothing. You just left."

Tears welled up in her eyes, "I can't take this anymore."

Michael looked at her and started crying. He rushed into the apartment and grabbed her tight. "I'm sorry," he repeated over and over again.

No words sprang from Mary's lips, telling him everything

would be okay. She'd been down this road too many times before and found herself without the energy or conviction to utter those words again. Instead, she just held him for a while.

Finally, she separated from him and walked over to close the apartment door. She turned toward Michael, wiping the remaining tears from her eyes. "Okay, Michael, you win. We'll sit down and talk. But you need to listen too. There's two fucking sides to this, remember?"

"I know," he responded quietly.

He sat down on the couch and she took a seat next to him.

"We can't keep going on like this," she said. "I know you're having a hard time dealing with stuff right now. But so am I. I've been there from the beginning when all of this shit first started, and every time you've run away and shut me out."

"I know," Michael said again, realizing that those two words had become a regular part of his vocabulary, "and I can't apologize enough. No one in this world means more to me than you. Maybe that's why I kept pushing you away? I didn't want to see you get hurt."

Mary looked at him for a moment, trying to gauge the sincerity of his words. "But that's the whole point, Michael. When two people are in love, they share the good times and the bad. They strengthen and build each other up and get through the hard times together. But you wouldn't let me in."

It was the first time Mary had used that word in a long time. A brief flare of hope ignited inside of Michael. "Does that mean you don't love me anymore?"

Mary was silent for a while before speaking. "I didn't say that," she breathed.

A glimmer sparkled in Michael's eyes. He grabbed her once more, but this time, instead of crying on her shoulder, he met her with a passionate kiss. At that moment, the final shards of terror and despair that had taken hold of him melted away completely. Love had conquered his evil.

Mary met his passion with a pang of desperate hunger, and for a long time, all they could do was clasp hold of each other and feel the once broken bond of love between them strengthen and heal itself anew.

Finally, Mary nuzzled Michael away, "This still doesn't fix everything."

He looked at her with new strength in his heart, "Hopefully what I have to tell you will."

Michael struggled at first with the words. How do you tell someone that you've been chosen to save the world from destruction, and that in a couple of days you are going to die so that the rest of the world can live?

Gabriel's voice popped into his head. *Just follow your heart, Michael.*

Michael took a deep breath and began, "Before you say anything, please hear me out completely. You probably won't believe me, but please try not to pass judgment until I've told you everything."

Mary nodded in agreement, albeit with a doubtful look in her eyes.

Michael was silent for a minute, but once he started, the rest poured from him as if a floodgate had opened. He told her everything, every little spec of detail he could remember. He recounted every nightmare to her in vivid detail.

When he told her about the torture Nybbas had put him through, he almost broke down again. But Mary put her hand on his reassuringly, calming him down. But when he told her about his role in the scheme of things, she grew defensive. "What do you mean, you're the chosen one?"

Michael grew fidgety. "You know I was adopted, right?"

Question marks flew into Mary's eyes. "Yes? Why?"

"The only thing I knew growing up was that my mother was adopted too. It turns out this pattern's been going on for some time."

"How long?"

Michael looked down at the floor. "Two thousand years."

Mary's jaw dropped. "Two thousand years? How do you know that?"

"Gabriel told me."

It took a minute for Mary to process everything, and when she did, her eyes misted over and her lips began to tremble. "And now you're telling me you're supposed to save the world?"

Michael could only guess at the hurt that pained her in that moment. "I didn't understand it at first," he said. "But as I replayed everything in my mind—all the shit that's happened to me—it all made sense."

At first, Mary didn't want to believe it—any of it. But the look in Michael's eyes told her that everything he had said was true. Her worst fears were coming true. Her eyes became misty as she spoke, "So, what happens now?"

Michael turned away from her and walked slowly to the little window that overlooked the street below. How could he possibly tell her now, that in two days he was going to die? He thought about running away again—his solution so many times in the past—but he knew that somehow, he had to find the strength to do the right thing. *What I wouldn't do for a hit of something right now!* But he tossed that thought quickly aside. He wasn't that person anymore. He couldn't be.

"Please, Michael, say something," Mary pleaded.

Then the words just spilled out, "Thursday night at midnight I have to die. Then, if all goes right, I'll come back again. Kind of like a resurrection replay."

Mary's eyes grew wide. "What did you just say?"

Michel grabbed her hands and held them tight. "When I come back, I'll lead the Chosen Ones against Belial and his Horsemen."

"But you said, if everything goes right? What does that mean?"

"It will," Michael said, trying to pour as much conviction into his words as he could. "It has to."

The words struck Mary like an arrow in her chest. Her lips trembled as she spoke. "No, you can't do this. You can't die now. I love you. You can't leave me like this."

She rushed at Michael and held him tight. She was on the verge of hysteria, crying uncontrollably. All Michael could do was hold her tight and let the pain pass.

"When this is all over, we can pick up right where we left off."

Finally, her crying subsided a little, and she could speak, "Why does it have to be you? Why can't someone else do it?" But she knew in her heart what the answer to that question was.

The two of them spent the night wrapped in each other's arms, afraid to let go; knowing it was their last together.

***

When Mary woke up the next morning, she was sad to find her bed empty and a note on the pillow that had held Michael's head the night before. In the middle of the night, Michael had slipped away quietly and left her to her dreams. Until recently, she would've accused him of running away again. But she knew this time was different.

She took a deep breath before opening the paper with trembling hands. She tried to remember that Michael was serving a higher power, but her heart still hurt. Slowly, she unfolded it.

Mary,

What can I possibly say to ease your pain right now? Nothing, except that I love you, now and forever.

They say love is blind, but I believe that it's more often the ones that are in love that are truly blind. Too many times, true love is lost in the cracks of our shallow lives as we go about our existence. It is only then when that love is stolen from us that we realize we've lost something special.

Most people don't get a second chance to appreciate that love. I'm one of the lucky ones. And, no matter how short that moment was, I feel as if we lived an entire lifetime together last night. I can't imagine loving anyone else.

Yours Forever,
Michael

Mary held the note close to her chest. She didn't cry frantically or shake uncontrollably. Everything that had happened had finally led her to a quiet place inside herself. Instead, she just whispered, "love you too, Michael."

Chapter 21

St. Anthony's Cathedral was a gigantic sprawling structure built in the mid-nineteenth century that spanned almost an entire city block. Vast towers spiraled toward the sky throughout the building, making it appear more like a fortress than a place of worship.

The large entrance door creaked loudly as Michael pushed it open. Immediately, a small burly man dressed in priestly robes came forward to greet him. "You must be Michael," the priest said with an eagerness in his voice. He shook Michael's hand firmly. "I'm Father Thomas. Please come in. Everything is ready for you."

Quickly and nervously, Father Thomas led Michael down the center aisle of the sanctuary toward the main altar. Under normal circumstances, Michael would've marveled at its architecture, with its massive columns and arches spanning the interior, its solid oak doors rising ten feet into the air, and the beautiful stained-glass windows that cast a myriad of rainbows throughout the immense sanctuary. But, these were not normal circumstances.

Father Thomas paused just long enough to make the sign of the cross at the altar before he veered to his right a short distance and opened a door that led to a small spiral staircase. Michael had to race to keep up with the man as he bounded up the steps. By the time they reached a small door five stories up, he was out of breath.

The priest reached into his robe and fished out a large key ring. A loud click preceded the squeak of the doors hinges as he opened the door to reveal the room beyond. He then stepped back to allow Michael access. "After you," he urged Michael.

Michael stepped nervously inside the small room and was shocked at its plainness. It was approximately ten feet square, with a bare wooden floor and a very low ceiling. The only window was a small stained-glass one on the east wall to let the rising sun shine through. A tiny cot rested against the west wall, with a large tapestry hanging on the wall above it, while the north wall was lined with candles placed upon a narrow altar.

"What's next?" Michael asked as he sat down on the cot.

"That's up to you," the priest replied.

Michael looked confused. "I don't understand."

"What I mean is that the next few hours are yours to spend any way you want. You can pray, meditate, sleep, or we can talk; whatever you wish."

Michael shifted uncomfortably on the cot.

"I can see that you're a little uneasy," Father Thomas said.

"That's putting it lightly. To be honest, I'm scared shitless right now." Michael said. Every bit of rational thought in his head was screaming for him to run away and leave this madness far behind. But, somehow, a little voice broke through the chaos, persuading him that he needed to stay and see this through.

"I could actually go for a little something to calm me down right about now."

Father Thomas replied simply, "Unfortunately, any substance you induce right now might lead to complications once we start the procedure."

Michael didn't like the sound of this being called a procedure, like he was getting an appendectomy or something. "It's just that...I don't feel right being here; like I don't deserve it or something. I feel like a hypocrite. My life is so fucked up, and I haven't been to church in years, yet I'm supposed to be some kind of savior?"

"Genuine faith does not come from a building made of stone or a book filled with written pages, Michael. Instead, it comes from what's inside a man's heart. A man's intentions go a long way toward his path to enlightenment. And while you've allowed certain influences in the past to cloud your judgment, I can see that you've always maintained a good soul."

The two of them spent the next couple hours discussing general religion and theology. Michael seemed desperate to understand, as if he still hadn't convinced himself of his worthiness, even though he had been assured repeatedly that he was.

After a while, the words slowly made sense and Michael became more at peace with himself. He understood things much more clearly...except what was to happen next. "I know this might be a stupid question, but how is it going to happen...my death and resurrection, and all?"

The priest thought about it for a moment. "At midnight, you will take part in a special communion. The 'flesh and blood' that you will consume during the ceremony will serve both to purify your soul from past sins and to sever the thread of life that binds you to this world. The communion wafer, representing the body of Christ, is laced with a very potent venom, while the wine, which represents his blood, is mixed with a strong tranquilizer, which will put you to sleep almost instantly. The experience should be painless and peaceful."

The entire conversation was strange. The way Father Thomas talked to Michael about his upcoming death in such a nonchalant manner was more than a little unnerving. "That takes care of the first part," he said, "but what about the important rising-from-the-dead part?"

Father Thomas dropped to his knees and pulled a bundle from beneath the cot. It was a slender item, about a foot long, wrapped in a blanket of yellowed linen.

He sat back down on the cot with the item balanced gingerly on his lap. He made the sign of the cross, chanting softly to himself, and then slowly unwrapped the mysterious object. A minute later, Michael was staring at an ancient and curious-looking dagger. He couldn't guess its age, but it disturbed him. A faint red hue caught his eye at the tip of the blade, and Michael wondered whose blood it had spilled.

At last, Father Thomas spoke. "Do you have any idea what this is?"

Michael shrugged. "It looks like an old knife to me. The real question is, what are you plan on doing with it?"

Father Thomas smiled, "This is no ordinary weapon, Michael. This dagger was fashioned from the spear-tip that pierced the flesh of Christ as he hung on the cross."

Michael was speechless.

The priest continued, "If you look closely, you can still see the bloodstains on its edge."

After a minute of stunned silence, Michael asked. "How in the world did you get that?"

"The spear was stolen from the soldier as he slept and has been kept hidden until now. It will provide you with the power needed to escape Death's grip."

Father Thomas continued, "After you've taken your last breath, I will press the tip of the weapon to each of the places on your body which parallel the wounds Christ suffered on the cross: your hands and your feet, your forehead and your side. The blood of Christ will flow from the weapon into your body to ignite the power inside you to defeat Death and rise again."

He then held up the cloth that had been wrapped around the knife. "Do you know what this is?" he asked.

Michael shrugged again.

"This is the Shroud of Turin—the fabric which covered Jesus' body as he lay in the tomb after his crucifixion. This will protect your soul as it crosses over."

Michael was puzzled. "Protect my soul? From what?"

Father Thomas replied, "There is a concern that Belial may try to claim your soul as you pass over into death."

"Say what?!"

"The concern is based upon a technicality," Father Thomas continued. "Belial may consider your sacrifice to be an act of suicide, which is named as the unforgivable sin. He will claim that it's no different from the deaths suffered at Jonestown or Heaven's Gate. Each of those individuals took their own life because of some belief or purpose given to them by another— a loophole that he'll try to exploit."

A wave of nausea hit Michael as he sat there in shock. "You mean to tell me that after everything that's happened, success or failure could depend on a fucking technicality?"

"In a sense, yes. But we must have faith that everything will turn out in the end."

"But now everything's changed," Michael said heavily. "Before, it was just a question of my faith; my convictions. Now it involves things much more complicated."

"No, Michael, things have not changed. This battle will still be fought and won through faith. Remember, you are not the only one involved in this struggle. You do not have to bear this burden on your shoulders alone."

A mighty roar of thunder tore through the night sky. A moment later, heavy rain pelted the roof of the tower with resounding force, while a howling wind whistled through the building.

Father Thomas looked toward the ceiling of the small room and closed his eyes, saying a silent prayer, before turning to Michael, "It's time."

Fear clouded Michael's eyes as he looked up at the stained-glass window pulsing with light from the storm outside. He turned his head toward Father Thomas and nodded solemnly.

Chapter 22

In some respects, Father Yehodi was a simple man. He dressed simply, ate simply, and lived simply. Worldly possessions meant nothing to him. But in other regards, he was ruthless. If he wanted something, he took it, not by brute force, but by careful manipulation. It wasn't complicated. That was how he'd come to be in his current position, using anything and everyone along the way to his advantage. Including the dead naked woman in his bed.

Her name was Symphony, or at least that was her stage name. That's all he knew, and that's all he wanted to know. Anything more was just useless information he didn't want cluttering his mind. He didn't actually care about the woman he'd just murdered. He just needed a little of her blood to go along with a bit of her soul.

Their lovemaking, the act itself unenjoyable, had been necessary to achieve what he wanted. Just as he'd neared the point of euphoria, he clamped his hands onto her neck and squeezed hard. She struggled to escape his grasp for a minute until his power proved too much, then she gasped one last time.

The timing had been perfect, allowing him to bask in her

death at the moment of eruption. He uttered a single word, 'manuari', just as her soul was leaving her body. Because of the violent nature of her demise, the curse would assure that a sliver of her spirit remained attached. That was all he needed.

While her body was still warm, he fished a knife out from beneath his mattress and cut a long incision just above her heart—the place where her soul was tethered to her body. As the blood bubbled freely from the cut, Father Yehodi reached up and plucked the glass eye from his left eye socket and slathered it in the blood.

For a moment he reminisced about when he had pledged his service to Belial—gouging his eye out with a spoon like he was removing the meat from a cantaloupe—and in return, he had been given special abilities that a normal person couldn't possess. Everything always came with a price, and in this case, the price was well worth it for him.

Once he had lathered up the orb sufficiently, he popped it back in and concentrated. An intense heat burned through his brain—searing white light that coursed through him—opening up his mind to the astral realm. After a moment, he found what he was looking for and a wicked smile spread across his lips.

The downside of using his special sight was that it drained him physically and left him exhausted. Once his vision was done, he fell onto the bed next to the dead woman and fell asleep on the blood-soaked sheets.

A series of thunder claps ripped through the night sometime later, snapping Father Yehodi out of his sleep. The voice of Belial hissed in his ear a moment later, "Have you found him?"

The priest jumped from the bed and fell to his knees. His voice came in quivers. "Yes, Master, he has been found. He is with Father Thomas at St. Anthony's."

"Good," Belial replied. "You know what must be done."

"It will be done as you have instructed, My Master. I will not fail you."

"I certainly hope not for your sake!"

Then the voice was gone, leaving Father Yehodi sitting on the floor drenched in a cold sweat. After a minute, he rose from his kneeling position and proceeded toward the dresser in the room's corner, where he found the barbed whip that was stained with his blood. He felt dirty and needed desperately to cleanse himself. Only then would he be worthy to complete his assigned task.

He pushed aside the rug in the middle of the room to reveal the emblem inscribed on the floor: a circle within a circle, with a skull in the middle—the seal of Belial.

He stepped into the center of the circle, bowed his head low, and began the ritual. As the barbs stung his flesh with each bite, he stood there, unflinching, drinking in the pain that would make him worthy again.

He continued his self-flagellation until the floor had become a pool of blood beneath his feet, and when he was satisfied that his penance was served, he showered quickly, dressed, and headed toward his destiny.

***

The tower trembled at the onslaught of the storm as Father Thomas looked up toward the ceiling, seeking strength from above. He handed the communion wafer to Michael and then recited a passage Michael hadn't heard since he was a child.

"And he took bread, gave thanks and broke it, and gave it to them, saying, This is my body given for you; do this in remembrance of me."

Michael looked at Father Thomas fearfully before taking a deep breath and plunging the wafer into his mouth. The sacrament tasted like cardboard but dissolved quickly. *I guess there's no turning back now.*

The priest handed a small gold chalice to Michael and continued, "In the same way, after the supper he took the cup, saying, This cup is the new covenant in my blood, which is poured out for you."

As the priest was speaking, Michael felt his body tingling and began to panic. *What the fuck have I done?*

He drank the sweet red liquid desperately and was rewarded with heavy eyelids before he even set the cup down on the altar.

A crackle of thunder and a flash of lightning seemed to announce the ceremony's conclusion. After helping Michael lay down on the cot, Father Thomas looked toward Heaven once more, "Almighty Father, it is done."

No sooner had those words escaped the priest's lips when a loud knock sounded on the tower's door. Father Thomas looked fearfully at Michael, who had slipped deeply under the influence of the sleeping drugs. He had thought that his presence and purpose this night were unknown to anyone else. Quickly, he pressed the tip of the blade into Michael's flesh at the designated areas as he uttered a series of silent prayers.

The priest remained quiet as another series of knocks resounded on the door, hoping the intruder would think the tower empty and leave. After a minute, a voice spoke up, "Father Thomas? Are you in there? It's me, Father Yehodi. Listen, I know what's going on in there, and I've come to warn you that you're in grave danger."

A second later, the door crept open. "In danger? From who?" Father Thomas asked worriedly.

"From me, you fool!" Father Yehodi cried as he pushed the door open hard, sending Father Thomas crashing to the ground in front of the cot. He walked in and casually surveyed the room.

"Quite a cozy little place you have here, Father. I hope I'm not disturbing anything important. If I am, I apologize. I assure you I'll be finished here soon."

He picked up the knife, which had clattered to the floor. "Is this what I think it is?" Father Yehodi asked.

Father Thomas didn't reply as he tried feebly to grapple the priest by the legs. Father Yehodi pushed him aside easily and smiled as he swiped the dagger through the air a few times, "Regardless of its place in history, or its 'supposed' holy significance, the real question I have for you, is how sharp is its blade? Can it still cut flesh the way it cut your precious Savior so long ago?"

He paused thoughtfully for a second, "I guess there's only one way to find out."

Father Yehodi bent down and plunged the blade deep into Father Thomas' chest with a tremendous thrust. The blade did indeed prove to be sharp enough, as it pierced flesh and bone to find the priest's heart.

Father Thomas looked at him in disbelief as he slumped to the ground. Like a fish out of water, his mouth opened and closed as he gasped for air through a fountain of blood that gurgled from his lips.

Father Yehodi walked over to where Michael's body lay, now only a breath away from death. He turned toward the dying priest once more, "How about something for dramatic effect?" he said. "This should look somewhat familiar to you."

He then leaned over and kissed Michael's cheek. Immediately, the image of Judas Iscariot jumped into Father

Thomas' mind. A burst of laughter flew from Yehodi. "I'm sure you see the irony of this moment."

Father Yehodi lifted the Shroud from Michael's chest and dangled it by one corner over a candle's flame until it ignited. He tossed it casually against the tapestry and in a matter of seconds, the entire room was engulfed in flames.

Father Yehodi quickly exited the room and headed back down the stairs toward the front entrance of the cathedral. As he walked outside, he looked up to see a deep red hue overtaking the night sky. He smiled as a flash of lightning streaked across the horizon.

Chapter 23

Darkness was an unwelcome visitor as it burst its way into Mary's apartment. A deep feeling of fear and dread attached itself to her core, and she felt a panic attack slithering right behind it.

She turned the switch on the lamp next to her. The brightness of the light made her squint for a second until her eyes grew accustomed to the change. She tried to rub them gently with her fingers but only winced in pain. The endless hours of crying throughout the day had left them dry and irritable.

She had read his letter at least a hundred times, each time hoping that the message would be different. But the words cut to her heart with the precision of a surgeon's tool every time she laid her eyes on them until it was all but gone. Finally, she resigned herself to the fact that their one night of true love was now just a memory she'd never experience again.

After a while, exhaustion overtook her, and she drifted off to sleep.

***

His voice woke her from a fitful sleep. "I couldn't do it, Mary."

Mary opened her eyes to find Michael sitting on the edge of her bed. His face was long and somber; his eyes deep and haunted.

She sat up in bed. "What do you mean?"

"I couldn't go through with it. When the time came for me to sacrifice myself, I chickened out and ran, just like I always do."

Mary snuggled up behind him. "Don't be so hard on yourself, Michael. They were asking you to do the impossible."

"Face it, Mary, I'm just a fuck-up. Always have been, always will be."

She grabbed his chin and turned his face toward hers, looking him in the eyes. "Hey, that's not true. So, you made some mistakes? Everyone has. Besides, I wouldn't love you if you were perfect. What would be the fun in that?"

Michael smiled, "You mean that?"

"Of course, I do."

He pushed her back down on the bed and straddled her. "Why don't you show me just how much you love me?"

She met his lips eagerly, grinding her body into his. But just as their passion rose to a fevered pitch, Michael paused.

He sat up and grinned a wide, toothy grin. "I have a confession to make."

"What in the world are you talking about?" Mary asked.

His face took on a sinister presence, "I lied to you."

At that moment, Mary knew. This was not her Michael anymore.

"I didn't run away, per se," he continued.

The shakiness in her voice was clear. "What do you mean?"

"What I mean is, I simply got a better offer and took it."

The fear growing on Mary's face fueled the enjoyment rising in Michael's. "I mean, it made sense when he explained it to me," he said.

Cold sweat formed on Mary's brow. "Who explained what to you, Michael?"

"Why, Belial, of course! He told me his entire plan. Said he'd give me anything I wanted if I help him. I told him I wanted you."

Mary started crying. "No, Michael! Please tell me you didn't do what I think you did?"

"What? Sell my soul? It's a small price to pay to be with the one you love."

Michael shot down until his face was inches from Mary's. "You did say you loved me, right?"

Mary laid there shaking, unable to answer.

"I'll take your silence as a yes," he said. "Now, it's time for us to be together forever."

Michael put his lips firmly to hers and pressed his full weight on top of her. She tried to struggle, but found herself unable to move. His body darkened until it was a black mass enveloping her. Then it slowly merged into her, swallowing her in its void.

**

With a desperate push, Mary forced herself awake and sat up in bed. The air was thick and ominous as it hung in the apartment, and the temperature felt like it had dropped at least twenty degrees since she had gone to sleep, bringing a deep chill running through her.

She looked at the clock on the bedside table and saw that it was almost midnight. Her already racing heart beat even faster.

A roar of thunder split the night seconds before a series of lightning flashes created a natural firework display that lit up the dark sky.

Mary rushed to the bedroom window and saw that the sky had turned a deep shade of red. The wind was gusting with the force of a hurricane, making even the strongest of trees bow at its power.

The window in front of her suddenly exploded inward, sending her flying backward across the room amidst a barrage of deadly glass missiles. She landed hard on the other side of the bed, feeling something inside her shatter from the impact. She yelled out in agony for a second and then felt herself slipping into unconsciousness. Her eye caught the clock on the table once more before giving in to the darkness. She saw that midnight had arrived, and with it, the end of the world.

Chapter 24

It started as a slight tremor, nothing more than a low rumble, followed by a slight shaking beneath Father Yehodi's feet. Seconds later, it grew into a massive earthquake that rocked the ground in all directions. He was just outside of the cathedral and watched as buildings along the street opposite crumbled and fell; vehicles were thrown around like Matchbox cars; while fire hydrants exploded, sending jets of water shooting like geysers into the sky.

The force of the onslaught sent the priest flailing to the ground. From his knees, he watched as the pavement before him writhed and buckled like a serpent coiling its way through the jungle in search of prey. A bolt of lightning struck the concrete only yards in front of him and the ground opened up. Smoke and fire leaped from the chasm as it spread its mouth wide. Seconds later, a figure emerged from the chaos.

Father Yehodi's voice trembled as he spoke. "Master," he said weakly.

"Rise, Yehodi," Belial said. "You have done well. Because of you, there's no way I can lose now."

Another roar rose from the chasm as the four Horsemen

flew out of the abyss and settled behind Belial. The skins of the Nightmares they rode upon were black as pitch, their eyes glowed evil red, and fire covered their hooves and replaced their manes. Each snort from the dark beasts brought a jet of smoke from their nostrils.

Belial beamed like a proud father as he looked at his creations. He then raised his right hand and pointed it at Father Yehodi. "As I promised, Yehodi, you will now be rewarded."

Immediately, the priest clutched his chest and fell to the ground. He looked up at Belial in disbelief. "Why, Master?" he gasped.

Belial kneeled close to the priest. "I'm giving you one more job to do, Yehodi. You will be the one to lead my children into battle."

Even as Belial spoke those words, the serpentine body of Pestilence darted from her steed and was upon the priest. Her reptilian mouth opened wide to expose its sharp, dripping fangs. A loud hiss preceded the deadly spray of acid that flew from her mouth and hit Father Yehodi full in the face.

The priest screamed and writhed on the ground as his skin melted from his skull. Smoke rose from his hair as it disintegrated, and soon the air was filled with the smell of charred flesh. Seconds later, the dead body of Father Yehodi lay still on the ground.

Belial opened his arms wide and yelled in a booming voice, "Rise, Yehodi, and take your place as Leviathan, the right hand of Belial."

A great whirlwind suddenly plucked the priest's body off the ground. A deep, red glow emanated from the heart of the tornado as flashes of electricity shot out in all directions. Then the chaos disappeared as suddenly as it had arrived, leaving a dark hulking mass on the ground resembling a giant egg-sack that writhed and pulsed as something inside sought to get out. Deadly claws ripped through the wall of the sack and a figure emerged.

The monstrous being towered above them. Standing nearly ten feet tall with leathery wings that spanned at least twice its height, Leviathan was even more terrifying than the Horsemen themselves. Long ivory horns chiseled to a deadly point adorned its head, sharp fangs extended from its twisted mouth, and a long, barbed tail snaked its way along the pavement, ready to strike. But what made it even more fearsome was the twisted face of Father Yehodi jutting from the middle of its chest, his lips moving slowly, as if trying to speak, or possibly to pray for salvation from the God he had betrayed.

Belial smiled and lifted his arms high into the air. "Let the destruction begin!"

The Horsemen shot into the air to signal the beginning of Belial's Apocalypse.

***

Fear wrapped around Michael like a serpent when he saw flames shooting from the tower as if it were a beacon, signaling that the end had begun. He knew if his body perished in the fire, their battle would be over before it even began. Belial would win and the world would die.

Before the fire could spread any further, though, a tremendous gust of wind encircled the tower. A moment later, the flames were extinguished and Michael's journey continued once more, as if he were being pulled upward by a tractor beam.

Suddenly, his ascent stopped.

He looked down in horror as a tentacle of black energy

wrapped itself around his legs and pulled him back down. *This is what Father Thomas warned me about!*

The tug-of-war that ensued threatened to destroy Michael. He cried out as he felt the fabric of his being strained beyond comprehension, tearing his soul apart. But just when he was sure he was going to end as broken in spirit as he had been broken in life, a burst of lightning ripped through the night and struck the black mass. The tentacle let out a loud screech as it writhed and convulsed before finally releasing its deadly grip.

Michael continued his ascent until a light engulfed him. He felt a tingling sensation course through him, like his whole body had fallen asleep in the wrong position. A moment later, the light subsided, and he stood in the middle of an enormous cavern with tunnels that branched off in several directions. The entire area was bustling with activity, as people rushed back and forth with a sense of purpose and determination etched on each one's face.

A familiar figure emerged and grabbed hold of him in a powerful embrace. "Welcome, Michael," Gabriel said happily. "I'd say that went better than expected."

Michael scoffed. "That's easy for you to say!" He looked curiously around, "Where are we?"

Gabriel replied, "The Dhankar Monastery, Northern India, or rather far beneath it. Consider this our base of operations, if you will."

Michael stood silent for a minute before speaking, "Are all these people...?"

"Angels? Yes."

Michael didn't know what to think. He'd certainly had his fill of crazy, but just when he thought he'd experienced everything, something new cropped up to surprise him. "How are we underground when I felt my spirit pulled upward?"

"As soon as your ascension was complete, you were teleported here. It happened so fast you didn't notice."

Gabriel took Michael's hand and led him forward. "Come with me. There's a lot to prepare and not much time to do so."

A short distance away, they came to a large crystal pool where several angels stood watching scenes play out in the water before them, like videos on a monitor.

A moment later, they were joined by four others, whom Michael recognized immediately. He looked at each one before looking down at the ground in shame. A flood of images came barreling back to his mind, reminding him of his failures. Ruth, Peter, Lucas, John—he had let them all down when they had needed him most.

Ruth came over and grabbed his hand. As he lifted his head, he saw a perfect expression of love smiling back at him. "Thank you, Michael," she said.

Michael replied, "For what?"

Lucas said, "It's because of you that we're here today."

"But I failed you."

"That's not true," Peter said. "You were willing to sacrifice yourself for each one of us."

John added, "That's what a leader does."

Michael stood there speechless as the pieces of the puzzle were finally coming together. The four individuals standing in front of him were all destined to be there, and as he looked at each one closely, a flurry of images suddenly flew through his mind: Ruth and her husband walking past him in a crowded airport as he prepared to board a flight; Lucas sitting at another table next to him at a restaurant while he was on a family vacation; Peter in a group photo while standing in front of Niagara Falls with a bunch of strangers;

and finally, John as part of the hospital staff rushing the gurney into the emergency room the day he had almost died.

His eyes grew wide in shock. "I've met all of you before!"

"Your lives have all been intertwined since the beginning," Gabriel said. "You were all destined to meet here today."

"But how did you know? And please don't say something like the Lord works in mysterious ways."

Before Gabriel could respond, Mary's name suddenly sprang to Michael's lips, and with it a knife to his heart.

He looked into the water fearfully as the scene suddenly shifted to Mary's tiny apartment. He saw her body lying motionless on the floor in a pool of blood. Softly, he whispered her name as he felt his spirit begin to crumble.

Chapter 25

Fierna crept through the dark corridors of Abriymoch, avoiding the eyes of the demons and the tortured souls. Her father was busy preparing his Horsemen for the final battle, and she hated him for it. Belial had promised her that they would rule Hell together, but the abominations were his new family now, while Fierna was nothing to him but a forgotten memory.

Only by stopping him could she hope to mend the relationship between them that he had so thoughtlessly thrown away. Fierna's heart raced as she contemplated her next move. Although she had faced Lucifer once before, the thought of facing him again made her shiver.

She took a deep breath and tried to calm herself down before proceeding. The stakes were too high for her to lose control. She could only hope that her determination and wit would be enough to succeed.

***

Fierna cursed under her breath when she spotted the two demon guards standing at the entrance to the labyrinth. They were colossal creatures standing well over eight feet tall, their skin a mottled gray with splotches of green and brown. Black ichor dripped from sharp fangs that jutted from their mouths, and their torsos were flanked with four long arms that ended in an array of deadly claws designed to tear through flesh easily. She had hoped to sneak in and avoid drawing attention to herself, but knew that was now impossible. The beasts would sense her approach instantly, regardless of whatever spell she may use. *So much for doing this the easy way*, she thought.

She took a moment to strategize, watching from behind a giant oak tree on the edge of the canyon as the sentries stood vigilant at the gate of the fortress. Nestled at the edge of a dense forest, Glasya's giant citadel stood as an impenetrable fortress against anyone foolish enough to encroach on its secrets. In the center of the lowest maze—a labyrinth of unfathomable length—stood the portal that would transport her to her destination. Unfortunately, the portal was closely guarded. So, not only did Fierna have to get past the demons at the gate, but she knew what waited for her far below and shivered.

Fierna took a shuddering breath and gritted her teeth, almost trembling from the force of her magic. The power within her welled up with an almost tangible heat that seemed to ripple off of her skin. When she opened her eyes again, they blazed like twin flames as she stepped out from behind the tree, an inferno of raw power crackling around her.

The demons spotted her immediately and roared in unison, their claws extending as they prepared to pounce. But Fierna was ready. She thrust her arm out in front of her, her fingers splayed wide as a stream of fire burst forth from her hand. The flames engulfed the closest demon, forcing it to back away with howls of pain as its skin sizzled and blackened. Quickly, she rushed forward with her sword drawn and impaled it through the chest, sending it crashing to the ground with a dying shriek.

Her momentary satisfaction was short-lived, however, as she felt sharp daggers rake across her back while she tried to roll away from the claws of the second beast. She brought her sword up to parry another attack, but the demon was too fast! One of its claws slashed across her thigh, while the third gouged a hole in her side. A loud cry flew from her lips as she fell to the ground amidst a volley of blood.

As the demon pressed in for a final blow, Fierna looked at it through eyes filled with a mixture of hatred and pain. *Okay, you ugly bastard! Time to end this!*

With a fierce yell, she pushed herself from the ground and threw her arm forward, sending a jet of fire into the chest of the creature. The creature staggered backward for a moment, giving Fierna enough time to swing her sword around. The blade bit deep into the demon's neck, sending its head crashing to the ground a second before the rest of its body followed suit.

Fierna slumped to her knees trying to catch her breath as she pressed her hand to her side to staunch the flow of blood. She concentrated for a second and a small flicker of flames engulfed her hand, filling the air with the sizzle of singed flesh as the intense heat cauterized the wound. She tried to bite back the scream before it left her lips, but failed. The cry was answered from somewhere inside the fortress as the alarm sounded. Time was running out.

Her breath was raspy and ragged as she sprinted towards the gate, her feet pounding against the rocky terrain. As she drew closer, she could see the intricate runes etched into the stone archway, each one pulsing with dark energy.

She knew there was only one way to get through the gate. Fierna slowed down and took a deep breath, her eyes scanning the runes for the correct sequence. She had committed them to memory, but it was always harder to perform under pressure.

The sounds of reinforcements drew closer as Fierna gritted her teeth and began to trace the runes in the air with her index finger, the magic emanating from her body enhancing her movements. Each rune glowed a bright blue as she traced it, and soon the entire sequence was complete.

With a deafening crack, the gate began to split apart down the middle, revealing a swirling vortex of blackness beyond. Fierna felt a chill run down her spine as she gazed into the abyss.

She took a deep breath and stepped forward, feeling the pull of the vortex as she was whisked away into the unknown. As her body was hurled through the vortex, Fierna felt the icy tendrils of fear creeping into her heart. She had been warned about the dangers that awaited her on the other side, but she had no choice. She had to do this, no matter the cost.

The vortex finally spat her out onto the floor of a dimly lit chamber, and Fierna scrambled to her feet, her eyes locked on the creature before her. It was a grotesque mass of floating flesh, a conglomeration of body parts all melded together, with orifices scattered throughout dripping bile and blood that sizzled when it hit the rocky floor. An overwhelming scent of decay covered the room like a thick blanket, stifling the air in her lungs as she struggled to breathe. Fierna could feel the demon's power radiating off of it in waves—ancient power that dated before even the creation of the Abyss—but she refused to back down. There was too much at stake.

A series of ear-splitting cries erupted from the demon—

high, piercing shrills emanating from the twisted mouths of a dozen cursed souls. Almost immediately, a wave of dizziness threatened to drop Fierna to her knees once more, but she fought through it, bracing herself with her sword.

Once the attack subsided, Fierna brought her sword up and charged the beast. As she held the blade high, searing pain tore through side once more. She looked down in horror to find her flesh bubbling and melting at the spot of her wound. A misshapen boil began to protrude from inside her, that quickly grew in size so that it jutted out of her like an extra limb. As the boils began to multiply, a series of black burn marks spread from the growth, engulfing her torso in a matter of seconds.

She knew she only had seconds before the decay would overtake her completely. Summoning all of her inner strength, Fierna channeled her magic into her sword, imbuing it with the power of fire. As she swung her weapon with what she knew would be her final attack, plunging her blade deep into the demon's frontal brain, flames erupted from the blade, engulfing the beast in a blaze of heat and light. The demon screamed in agony, its body dissolving into ash and smoke. As it died, the decay receded from Fierna's body until she was whole again.

Fierna fell to her knees, panting from the exertion, while the chamber began to crumble around her.

When the dust finally settled, she found herself standing at the mouth of the maze, the darkness inside whispering its deadly curse in her ears. *Now comes the hard part*, she thought bitterly.

Chapter 26

The moment Fierna stepped around the corner, a deathly hiss echoed throughout the passage. She had no time to think as she saw the multitude of arrows racing toward her like fiery meteors. With only a split second to react, she flung herself forward to escape certain death. Pain exploded in her shoulder when one of the speeding missiles finally hit its mark. "Damn it!" she cursed through gritted teeth.

Fierna gathered herself to her knees and yanked the arrow from her shoulder, bringing another howl from her lips. Determined to go on, she pulled herself up and continued down the corridor until she came to another intersection. She cautiously peered down both corridors before turning left and pressing on. The further she went, the colder and thinner the air became, making each step feel like it was taken in a dark abyss of despair. Lead weights seemed to anchor her feet to the ground, giving her the sensation of walking an endless void.

Fierna pushed on through the eerie atmosphere, her heart pounding in her chest. She couldn't shake the feeling that she was being watched, or worse, hunted. The thought of being killed in this place sent shivers down her spine, but she couldn't turn back now. She had to keep moving, no matter the cost.

The passage seemed to stretch on forever, with no end in sight. Fierna's footsteps echoed loudly off the cold stone walls, a constant reminder of her isolation. She could feel her fear growing with each step, threatening to overwhelm her.

As she rounded another corner, she found herself face to face with a figure cloaked in darkness. Her heart leaped into her throat as she realized that this was what she had been afraid of; the thing that had been following her. It stepped forward, revealing a face twisted with malice and eyes that glowed with an otherworldly light.

Fierna stood frozen as the figure let out a low, guttural growl, and she knew she had to act fast. She felt her heart racing in her chest, adrenaline pumping through her veins. This would be a fight to the death, and she was ready to do whatever it took to survive.

The creature lunged forward, its claws glinting in the dim light. Fierna slid to the side, bringing her sword down in a swift arc. The creature dodged her attack, swiping at her with its claws. Fierna ducked under its outstretched arm, rolling to the side and coming up on her feet. She swung her sword again, this time hitting the creature squarely in the chest. It let out a horrific scream, its body convulsing as it fell to the ground.

She looked at the creature for a moment as the death twitches coursing through its body slowly subsided. Finally, when she was sure the thing was dead, she stepped around it and began down the corridor.

Then she heard a shuffling noise behind her. Fierna turned around to see the demon shambling back to its feet. "You got to be fucking kidding me!"

Before the creature could gather itself for another attack,

she raced forward and swung her sword around, slicing its head off. "Let's see you come back from that, you ugly fuck!"

When the thing refused to move again, she wiped the sweat from her forehead and continued down the passage. As she walked, she noticed the walls begin to change. Instead of cold, gray stone, they were now covered in intricate carvings of an ancient language. Using her knowledge of the language, she began to decipher the carvings. Fierna's heart raced with anticipation.

She pressed on, following the symbols deeper into the passages. The air grew even colder, and she could see her breath misting in front of her. She was close.

Finally, Fierna saw the portal in the distance, its flickering blue light illuminating the darkness. As she approached, a sense of relief washed over her, but that relief was short-lived when a voice whispered in her ear, sending shivers down her spine. "You do not belong here, Fierna. This place is forbidden, even for you."

Fierna spun around with her sword held firmly, but there was no one there.

"Who are you?" she demanded, her heart pounding as she looked around frantically.

Hideous laughter echoed throughout the corridor, assaulting her senses from everywhere, all at once. A wave of fear washed over her. "I didn't come here to cause trouble," she said, trying to keep her voice steady. "Just let me pass and I won't have to do anything drastic."

The hideous laughter instantly turned to a maddening howl that seemed to rise from the depths of the abyss itself. A second later, sharp claws raked across her back from her unseen foe. She spun around quickly, swinging her sword wildly, hoping to connect with the creature, but found only empty air.

Another attack by the invisible being found the soft flesh of Fierna's abdomen, and she cried out in pain as she fell to her knees. Her pain was quickly replaced with burning hatred. "Okay, whoever the fuck you are, don't say I didn't warn you."

She looked up from the floor, her eyes shining like raging infernos, while her hair erupted into tentacles of fire that shot out in all directions, lighting up the corridor with the power of the sun. A chorus of loud hisses emanated from the serpent-like flames as they sought out their target.

Seconds later, a loud shriek sounded an instant before a figure materialized in front of her. As its form solidified, a loud gasp flew from Fierna's lips. Her mind immediately raced back to her mother's death. She could still hear Naome's dying breath echoing in her ear; could see the pool of blood spreading from the wound in her chest, turning the ground beneath her a deep shade of red. When she looked up to see her mother's killer escaping into the shadows, the same face looked back at her then that was smirking at her now.

"You!" Fierna shouted as she jumped to her feet. "You're going to pay for what you've done!"

The figure was tall and slender, shrouded in a dark cloak that flowed as if it was made from shadows themselves. Its face was long and pointed with dark hair that provided a hood that nearly covered its piercing eyes. "I assure you, Fierna, as was the case back then, my presence here today is merely business."

"Who sent you?"

"You know I can't divulge that information," the dark assassin replied.

"Then I guess I'll have to rip the answer from your dying lips as I split you open!"

"You can try."

"Oh, I'll do more than try!" she said before she launched herself forward, catching the Dogai assassin off-guard. Her blade slashed across his mid-section before he had a chance to react, sending him crashing to his knees.

She spun quickly around with another wide swing, but this time her blade found empty air, as the assassin vanished quickly into the shadows once more. With her energy depleted from her recent fiery outburst, Fierna scanned the area carefully, trying to avoid a deadly, hidden attack that could end everything before it even started.

A soft rush of air whispered into her ear a split second before she spotted the blood dripping to the floor just in front of her. Quickly, she spun to her right and thrust her sword violently upward. The blade sunk eagerly into the flesh of the assassin, embedding itself so deep through the chest, that the tip extruded from its back.

"I warned you," Fierna said as the figure materialized before her, his mouth gasping for air as black blood bubbled between its lips. "Now tell me who sent you," she pressed.

"You...already know," the assassin said weakly before he closed his eyes and died.

With a violent yank, Fierna pulled her sword from the assassin's body, allowing it to crash to the ground.

As the words repeated themselves in her head, her anger grew. She knew who had sent him alright, and now, more than ever, she was determined to make him pay!

Chapter 27

Fierna stepped through the portal, leaving the labyrinth behind. As she emerged on the other side, her growing anger was immediately replaced with a deep sense of foreboding. Now that she was in the ninth circle of Hell, she knew that danger lurked around every corner. She would need to stay on her guard if she had any chance to survive.

Suddenly, she heard a noise up ahead. It sounded like someone was talking, and the voices were getting louder. Fierna crouched down, hiding behind a nearby pillar.

Peering around the corner, she spotted a group of demons gathered in a circle, their voices rising in excitement as they discussed something that seemed important. Fierna couldn't make out what they were saying, but she could sense a dark energy radiating from them.

Taking a deep breath, Fierna stood up and stepped out from behind the pillar and charged towards the group of demons, her own demon powers pulsing through her veins. The demons turned towards her, snarls forming on their faces as they realized they were under attack. But Fierna was quick, launching herself into the fray with a ferocity that took the demons by surprise.

Fierna's magic crackled around her as she summoned flames that incinerated demon after demon with a flick of her wrist. Her sword became a harbinger of death in her hand as she swung it around with deadly ferocity. The battle was intense and brutal, but Fierna fought with everything she had. She was both weary and battered by the time the last demon fell.

With a renewed sense of purpose, Fierna continued on her journey through the ninth circle of Hell, determined to make her way to the heart of Lucifer's realm. She knew that she had a long and arduous road ahead of her, but she was ready for whatever lay ahead. Her father had betrayed her, and he would pay for what he had done. And if that meant becoming something darker and more ruthless than she ever thought possible, then so be it.

***

As she approached Lucifer's throne room, Fierna felt a sense of dread wash over her. Taking a deep breath, she stepped forward, her eyes locked on Lucifer's imposing figure. He towered over her, his eyes cold and calculating as he studied her. Fierna met his gaze head-on, refusing to back down.

"Fierna!" Lucifer said. "I'm surprised to see you here. You're either braver than I thought, or a bigger fool."

Fierna's mind raced back to a time of chaos, when the most powerful demons sought to overthrow Lucifer and take control of the Nine Hells. She had been duped and persuaded by Azazel to join him in his own plot to usurp the King of Hell. When Azazel's forces were annihilated, he quickly left Fierna to fend for herself. It was only through Belial's pleading that she escaped an eternity of endless torture.

"I've come to make a deal," she said, her voice steady

despite the fear that threatened to consume her. "I want my father's head on a platter, and I'm willing to do whatever it takes to make that happen."

Lucifer raised an eyebrow, a smirk playing at the corner of his lips. "After everything he's done for you, you would betray him like this?"

"He's the one who's betrayed me!"

"So? What makes you think I'd help you?" he asked, his tone mocking.

"Because I'm not the only one he's betrayed."

Lucifer raced forward and grabbed her by the throat, lifting her high in the air. "You better not be playing with me, Fierna! Belial was my most trusted general. Dishonoring his name is enough cause for me to rip your spine out, and he's not here to save you this time."

Fierna's heart pounded in her chest as she struggled to breathe. "I can prove it," she gasped.

Lucifer looked at her for a moment and then eased his grip on her, ever so slightly.

"Please," Fierna pleaded. "Let me show you."

After an agonizing minute, Lucifer finally released his grip on her and she tumbled to the ground.

"Tell me what you know," Lucifer said impatiently.

Fierna took a deep breath, "Belial plans to start his own apocalypse, claiming that you are behind the scheme, and then present himself as a savior to stop you and regain entrance into Heaven."

Lucifer's eyes widened in surprise. "That's quite the scheme, Fierna. You claimed to have proof?"

Fierna nodded, her heart pounding in her chest. She reached into her bag and pulled out a small, ornate box that she opened to reveal a single piece of parchment inside.

"This was written by Belial's hand," she said, holding the

parchment out towards Lucifer. "It outlines his plans in detail, and it's all the proof you need to see that he's been plotting against you."

Lucifer took the parchment from Fierna's outstretched hand and read it over carefully. Fierna watched as his expression shifted from disbelief to anger.

"This is unacceptable," he said, his voice low and dangerous. "Belial will pay for his treachery."

Then Lucifer turned his attention back to Fierna. "And as for you, while this does absolve you somewhat for your trespass, you still came into my domain uninvited. Do not do so again. Next time I won't be so forgiving."

As she shrunk away from Lucifer, Fierna felt a sense of satisfaction wash over her. Her plan had worked—she had successfully turned Lucifer against her father and secured her revenge. Maybe, then finally, Belial would accept his fate and they could begin to mend their relationship? She knew it was a fool's errand, but it was her only hope.

Chapter 28

Like lightning, the five warriors streaked across the sky, sparks flying from the hooves of the Nightmares, leaving a trail behind each one like the tail of a comet as it sped through the endless reaches of space.

Within minutes, they were hovering over the Mediterranean Sea a few miles north of the Gaza Strip.

War led the charge as he swooped down on his death-horse toward Bethlehem.

The streets surrounding Manger Square were silent; the air filled with an uneasy dread. Nothing stirred. Nothing moved. It was as if a spell had been cast over the entire town, paralyzing everyone.

Behind Manger Square stood the Church of St. Catherine and, beyond that, the Church of the Nativity. Both were unsuspecting victims in the Unholy War that was about to begin.

The ground trembled beneath the behemoth as he landed in front of the Square. He dismounted and strode to its center. Then, with a mighty swing, he brought his giant battle-ax down upon the sacred stone. A large crack formed in the ground as the earth split in two by the force of his blow. A low rumble reverberated through the area just before the ground convulsed.

***

The quaint little two-bedroom house stood silent about twenty yards back from the road on Ash Salon Street. It belonged to Saadya and Allonia, who had purchased the home shortly after finding out Allonia was pregnant. Because of its proximity to the YMCA nearby, where Allonia worked as a guidance counselor, and its relatively straightforward route to the Church of the Nativity, a place they frequented regularly; it quickly became the perfect setting for their growing family.

The night was eerily quiet, until Daliah let out a loud wail that seemed to pierce right through Saadya's heart. He had done everything he could think of to soothe the little one, but even his best efforts were for naught. He knew in his heart that nothing would stop her cries until Allonia came home from work. He prayed she wouldn't be too late or else his sanity might be lost forever. The clock seemed to tick by slowly as he waited, fighting the urge to pull out what few strands of hair were left on his head.

"Thank God, you're home!" he said as he met her at the door. "I've tried everything, but she won't stop crying."

Allonia chuckled as she put her purse on the table and held her arms out for her daughter. "Here, let me have her."

Saadya handed Daliah to his wife, who gently placed her over her left shoulder. Almost immediately, a loud 'burp' escaped the child's lungs.

"Well, apparently you didn't try burping her," she said with a smile.

Saadya grew a little embarrassed before becoming

frustrated. It was true. The thought hadn't crossed his mind. *How can I be so stupid!* he thought bitterly.

Allonia kissed him lightly on the cheek, sensing his frustration. "Don't be too hard on yourself. It's not like children come with instruction manuals, after all."

"I know. I just want to do my best to help with her."

"You are, dear. Trust me."

Within seconds, after Daliah had expelled the air bubble from her lungs, she closed her eyes and was fast asleep.

Allonia whispered, "Let me put her to bed and I'll be right back."

Saadya nodded and watched with a smile as she left. She was the perfect mother and the perfect wife. Her natural maternal instincts, coupled with her kind heart, made him the happiest man on earth. He couldn't imagine life without her, nor did he want to.

While Allonia was busy tucking their daughter in for the night, he figured he'd take advantage of the opportunity to relax for a few minutes and glance through the newspaper. If past routines held, he'd have about twenty minutes to himself as she rocked Daliah for a while to make sure she was sound asleep.

He had no sooner sat down in his recliner, with the Gaza Weekly opened on his lap, when a low rumble sounded through the house a moment before the structure shook. It only lasted a few seconds, and when it was done, he bolted from his chair toward the nursery.

The tremor had woken Daliah from her sleep, and he could hear her screaming down the hall, but before he could reach the doorway, another tremor tore through the area, this time with enough force to knock Saadya to the floor.

He watched in horror from his prone position as the house swayed back and forth as if caught on a giant tidal wave. He could feel blood dripping from a cut on his head where he had hit the wall when he fell. But that didn't matter at the moment. His only thought was to save his family!

Allonia yelled out to him, "Saadya!?" echoing Daliah's cries of panic.

Even though she was only a few feet away, her voice sounded weak and distant above the clamor of the earthquake that continued to shake the house to its foundation.

"Hold on, Allonia!" he yelled. "I'm coming! Get somewhere safe!"

Before she could respond, he heard a loud, thunderous crash, and then she and their baby were silent. His heart sank as he imagined the worst.

"Allonia!?" he cried out.

There was no answer.

Then, a moment later, the rest of the house collapsed, and Saadya joined his wife and daughter in silence.

***

Outside, the earth trembled like an angry god, shaking the foundations of buildings and sending terrified people into the street. Screams erupted through the air as families scrambled for safety, some carrying the broken bodies of those who hadn't made it out in time toward what they thought would be safety.

They were wrong.

There would be no shelter to escape the disaster. The earthquake was just the beginning. What followed turned the area into a war zone. A series of deafening explosions filled the sky as broken gas lines went up in flames, littering the countryside with ash and carnage. In mere seconds, everything had been engulfed in a raging firestorm. The flames wrapped around the buildings like greedy fingers and crawled up into the sky behind them.

Pleased with his work, War jumped back on his dark steed and charged through the Square toward the Church of St. Catherine. As he rode, balls of fire flew from the mouth of the Nightmare, turning the sacred Square into a huge bonfire that served as a signal to the world that the end was near.

The giant battle-ax whirled from his hand like a missile, obliterating the entrance door of the church as if it were made of paper. The sound echoed through the night like a cannon blast, sending shivers of terror down the spines of all who heard it. His face lit up with a feral grin when he saw men cowering in fear at his approach.

The Nightmare wasn't done yet. A second later, flames licked hungrily at the velvet drapes that hung along the walls as shards of glass shot outwards from the windows blown apart by scorching heat.

He glanced over at the giant crucifix that hung behind the altar, and with one ultimate gesture, he reared back and heaved his ax forward. The sound of cracking wood filled the air as the symbol crashed to the ground with a resounding boom, finishing off the holy place once and for all—a final stamp on the sacred building's destruction.

Making his way to the Church of Nativity, he descended from his steed and marched toward the nativity scene outside. With one swift movement, his ax ripped through the display, scattering the broken wooden figures onto the dirt below. An eerie silence descended once more on the area as a soft rain began to sprinkle down from above, like the angels were silently weeping at the destruction. War chuckled at the thought.

He was disappointed to find the sanctuary empty except

for a woman cowering in the corner, but when he drew near, he saw she was shielding something from him.

"No, please no," she cried desperately.

He swiped her away to reveal a little girl, approximately six years old, huddled low and crying. A smile crossed his lips as he reached down and scooped up the woman. Holding her high in the air, he squeezed her throat tightly. Then a loud snap signaled the woman's death.

He bent his face down close to the little girl. "Today's your lucky day, girl," he said. "Tell everyone you see that the War to End All Wars has started."

Chapter 29

The darkness surrounding Mary was absolute, suffocating the life from her. Panic surfaced in her mind as she tried to open her eyes, only to discover they were sealed shut by some sticky substance. Desperately she willed herself to move her arms and legs to no avail; only her head and neck seemed to have any sense of mobility.

Then she remembered the storm. She remembered the howling tempest as it crushed its way through the alley alongside her apartment building. She remembered the explosion of glass that had sent her sprawling backward. And she remembered the feeling of bones shattering inside her as she hit the floor.

Now she lay there blind and paralyzed; helpless and alone. The only small comfort she had was that her shattered vertebrae prevented her from feeling any pain.

Knowing that she was beyond the hope of rescue; no prince charming to save her—her prince already sacrificing himself to fight a nobler battle with a higher purpose—or no emergency room savior with a magical scalpel to make her whole again; Mary let her mind and spirit sink into a state of emptiness.

As she surrendered to the darkness, she said a silent prayer for Michael, hoping that her last thoughts would help him in his struggle against Belial's evil scheme and give him the strength he needed to defeat the bastard.

Then she gave herself up completely. Death would be her ultimate savior.

***

Michael slunk to his knees as a wave of anguish washed over him.

Gabriel whispered something to one angel, who departed immediately.

"Do not despair, Michael," Gabriel said as he placed his hand on Michael's shoulder. "Have faith in your purpose, focus on the battle to come, and believe with every ounce of your soul that we will win in the end."

Michael tried. Even in the presence of the Archangels, he found himself unable to surrender to their conviction. *How can I find the strength to defeat Hell when everything right in the world has been ripped apart?*

***

Hanging desperately from the splintered remains of the window casing, the final fragment of glass was both a testament to the frailty of human life and the strength of its will. Precariously it hung, as if by a thread, while its brethren lay scattered around the room in a million jagged fragments.

As the darkness dissolved and consciousness took hold once more, Mary's eyelids fluttered slightly, breaking through the crust that had sealed them shut earlier. The sound of glass falling to the bedroom floor snapped her mind back to full comprehension. The final splinter had given in to its struggle to remain defiant and had joined its brothers and sisters in subjugation on the bedroom floor.

Her first thought was disappointment. The finger of Death had failed to sever the silver thread that held her to this life. She supposed she would die eventually, but she had selfishly hoped it would be swift and painless. Instead, she lay on her back staring at the ceiling through eyes quickly filling up with tears. She was completely helpless against whatever might come next.

From her vantage point, she could see just above the shattered window, where the darkness was giving way to the light of the coming dawn. In the past, Mary had marveled at the miracle of the rising sun, letting the warmth and energy bath her as she stood in front of the window each morning. But now, her mind swimming with thoughts of death and despair, each new sun would instead signal another day of torment and anguish.

At first, Mary didn't grasp the fact that the world around her was filling with light much faster than a normal sunrise. Soon, the intensity of the light was so bright she couldn't keep her eyes open. Even then, with her eyes clamped shut, tiny teardrops spilled from their corners.

A terrible thought entered her head, telling her that the end of the world had arrived. The nuclear holocaust that so many had feared their whole life, had finally happened, brought on by Belial's evil. It wasn't concern for her own life that made her sad; it was the millions of innocent lives that would be lost that overwhelmed her.

A slight buzzing noise then caught her ear. And as she listened harder, the sound became more of a humming.

A figure stepped out of the center of the light and approached her. With each step, the surrounding hum transformed until it grew into a chorus.

The face of the angel held her mesmerized, extinguishing the horrible thoughts from her mind. Words echoed in her head, bringing comfort. *Do not be afraid, Mary. The Lord's grace shall protect you. Your time—your destiny to serve a higher purpose—has not yet come.*

The angel placed one hand on her heart and one on her stomach. She felt a warm, tingling sensation coursing through her body as the bones in her spine were fused back together. Then the angel took his hand from her chest and placed it on her forehead.

"Sleep now," he said.

Chapter 30

The sky wept, and all of Jerusalem was plunged into darkness. A deafening roar shook the ground on the outskirts of the city as Pestilence descended, her monstrous form blotting out the starlight. Her crimson scales glowed like a funeral pyre, while a chilling hum emanated from her throat. Without hesitation, she reared up and slashed off her own tail with a single swipe of her razor-sharp claws.

Black liquid spurted from the wound before it sealed shut, and an instant later a new appendage had regrown in its place. The severed tip lay wriggling on the ground like some putrid earthworm, then suddenly melted into a black puddle that quickly multiplied. Thousands upon thousands of slimy creatures spawned from this strange ooze, quickly forming an army of insects that marched toward the Holy City.

***

Pashme was hoping tonight would be different. It had been a long time since her and Daniel had spent any quality time together, the demands of their jobs leaving them both exhausted each night without even enough energy to pretend they were married. Not that they resented each other, or had fallen out of love. They were just tired. Completely and utterly exhausted.

She had vowed, though, not to become like her parents, cold and alone, even though they lived in the same house and slept in the same bed.

Pashme had even taken the day off from work to prepare a special night, something she'd never done before. As soon as Daniel got home, she planned to surprise him, first with his favorite meal—Shakshuka, spiced with paprika and cayenne pepper, with just a bit of nutmeg, followed by honey baklava for dessert; and then a bottle of Golan Heights Syrah to get him in the mood. If everything went as she hoped, it might rekindle a little bit of their fire.

The look on Daniel's face was priceless as he walked into the dining room and saw the candle-lit dinner.

"What's the special occasion?" he asked as he sat down at the table.

"Besides the fact that I have the best husband in the world?" Pashme replied.

Daniel chuckled, "Now, it sounds like you're trying to butter me up!"

It was Pashme's turn to laugh. "No, I just thought it was time for us to enjoy ourselves a bit. We've both been working so hard."

Daniel's head lowered a little, the reality of his neglect setting in. He had fallen into a deep trap that so many others had perished in before. He had put work before love.

He looked her in the eyes, "I'm sorry."

A soft tear gathered in the corner of Pashme's eye that she brushed away. "I didn't say that to make you feel bad. I just know how hard you've been working lately and thought you might enjoy a nice meal."

He lifted her chin gently, "If this Shakshuka is any sign, then a good meal isn't all I'll be enjoying."

"Just eat your food before it gets cold," Pashme said with a smile. "Then we can work on dessert."

Every bite he took was a slice of heaven; every sip of wine a journey to euphoria; and every wink of her eye a flame in his heart.

After the meal, he did something that he hadn't done enough of in recent months. He made love to her; heated, passionate love, where he explored every inch of her body with tenderness and ferocity until they were both drenched in sweat and out of breath. Then they snuggled together until they both drifted off to sleep.

A buzz in Daniel's ear woke him up sometime later. He swatted at the insect to shoo it away, but it persisted with a vengeance. Finally, unable to avoid the pest, he sat up in bed and turned on the light.

The jostling woke Pashme. "What's wrong?" she asked.

"There's a bug in here," he replied.

"Just ignore it and come back to bed. It'll go away."

"I can't just ignore it. You know how I am. I'll never be able to get back to sleep unless I know it's gone."

He leaped out of bed, blindly grabbing for anything that might help protect him. His fingertips grasped one of his house-shoes, and when he spun around, ready to face his intruder, a chill ran through him. Occupying the air near the window, their movements in perfect harmony like a cobra preparing to strike, was a menacing swarm of giant hornets— at least a hundred—and they were all trained on Daniel.

With a desperate cry, he screamed out to Pashme, "Run!" yet his warning fell on deaf ears as half of the mass suddenly split from the group to encircle Pashme in bed.

In an instant, they were both surrounded by beating wings

and sharp stings. In a terrifying explosion of pain, Daniel and Pashme lay frozen in pools of blood and green puss—their bodies and minds forever silenced.

***

The sounds outside were intermittent at first: a dog scavenging for food yelped for a second and then was silent; a baby's cry was extinguished quickly before mom and dad could hear its anguish; the sound of a man flailing wildly at an unseen foe before crashing to the floor of his bedroom.

Then, ear-shattering screams pierced the night in rapid succession. People charged out of their homes, screaming in terror, desperate to escape the savage insect attacks.

Pestilence smiled and slithered onto her steed's back, urging it high into the sky. Floating miles above the city, she opened her mouth wide and a jet of greenish gas shot forward, creating a noxious cloud hovering over the center of the city. She urged her steed around the perimeter of the cloud in a counter-clockwise circle, expanding the circumference of her orbit and increasing her velocity until she was nothing more than a blur streaking through the sky. Before long, the gaseous mass hung like a glowing green shadow encompassing more than twenty square miles.

A roar erupted from the Nightmare before a barrage of fireballs flew from the creature's mouth. One after another, they penetrated the green mist until the entire mass began spewing acid rain upon the citizens of Jerusalem far below.

Quickly, Pestilence raced down to Old City—considered by some to be the center of the world—and watched in delight as people scurried outside to escape the insect attack, only to have their flesh burn and melt away as the deadly rain poured down on them from above.

Then she spotted a little girl huddled in the corner of a small porch. Her mother's dead body lay before her in a pile of smoking green mucous.

She slithered from her steed and was upon the girl in the blink of an eye. Acid dripped from her mouth as she hissed at the girl, sending small jets of smoke into the air as it ate away at the wooden porch, "Are you afraid, little girl?"

The girl nodded fearfully.

"Good! Now tell the rest of the world that Hell is coming for them!"

Chapter 31

Michael turned away from the pool. He couldn't watch anymore. Every second tore him apart.

"Look again at the waters, Michael," Gabriel said a moment later, "and realize that with Him all things are possible."

Michael reluctantly turned back toward the pool and was surprised to see the angel healing Mary's broken body. "I thought the angels weren't supposed to intervene in the natural course of things?"

"They aren't. But sometimes a situation arises that goes against this natural course. At these times, the guardian angels spring into action to save those souls from premature death. That same situation applies here. Because of this, we're able to intercede. Now she'll be free to fulfill her destiny."

"Destiny?" Michael asked.

"Look closer, Michael. See with your heart, not with your eyes."

It took Michael a second, but then he saw it. There, in the middle of Mary's aura, was a tiny speck of light, brighter than the light surrounding it.

He looked at Gabriel in surprise.

"Yes, that's your unborn son, Michael."

Tears fell from Michael's eyes, but unlike before when he thought he'd lost everything, this time they were tears of joy.

Gabriel continued, "Just know, his life will be one of love and salvation."

For the first time in his life, Michael had a reason to fight. Scratch that. He had two reasons to fight! "Why can't I lead the Chosen One's now before the Horsemen cause any more damage?"

"Your body isn't ready yet. If you returned now, the poison would still be too strong."

Michael asked, "But I still don't understand? Why do I have to be resurrected?"

"The black orb inside each of the Horsemen's chest contains the last remaining essence of that person's soul. Although Belial is powerful, one thing he cannot do is create life. If these orbs are removed from their host, that body will die and the soul will ascend into the light where it belongs. This release can only happen at the hands of one chosen and anointed by God. Therefore, we must wait for your body to heal."

Gabriel motioned for Michael to follow as he exited through a side tunnel. A minute later, they were in another large chamber, where Azrael was talking to a large group of angels.

"Michael," Azrael said, "I've been waiting for you. I have some gifts that should help you in battle."

He held out his hands, and a suit of armor made of a very lightweight golden mesh materialized. "This suit of armor will repel anything the Horsemen throw at you."

Michael put on the armor as Azrael held out his hands once more, manifesting a brilliant golden helm. "This is the Helm of Truth, designed to separate reality from illusion."

"The last gift I have for you, Michael, is this." He held out his hands one last time and a peculiar-looking sword appeared. Embedded inside its glistening blade, at the base of the hilt, was a familiar-looking dagger.

"I know that blade," Michael exclaimed. "Father Thomas showed it to me before he was killed. He told me it was made from the spear that had been thrust into Christ's side as he hung on the cross."

"That is correct, Michael."

Azrael held the sword up high. "Father Almighty, anoint your servant, now!"

The sword glowed brilliantly white as Azrael held it above his head. "Step forward, Michael, and receive that for which you have proven yourself worthy."

Michael hesitated for a second, still battling his internal feelings of worthiness. Finally, he stepped forward as instructed.

The sword glowed even brighter as Azrael brought it down and plunged it into Michael's side.

Michael's eyes widened in panic and shock as he was lifted off the ground, his body contorting into a shape that mirrored Christ on the cross. His arms outstretched with palms facing outward and his feet stacked one on top of the other. All around his body a dazzling golden light shone from each of Christ's wounds, searing Michael's skin like red-hot irons as all his sins were slowly burned away. The light grew brighter until it was too much to bear, and soon he was nothing but a whirling mass of spinning energy.

The spinning suddenly ceased, and Michael collapsed to the floor sobbing uncontrollably. He looked up, tears staining his face, and whispered, "I understand everything now."

Chapter 32

Famine limped through the empty streets of Nazareth, with pieces of him breaking off and disintegrating with every step he took. The scraps of his rotting corpse left behind gushed with blood, attracting legions of wriggling maggots that flourished upon what was left of him. The Horseman would occasionally stop and thrust out his arms, unleashing a barrage of inky specks that darted forward like missiles. Smaller than fruit flies, these tiny winged creatures moved as if they were guided by some unseen force, targeting anything that dared to cross their path.

***

Uri lay motionless in his bed, unaware of the dark entity that had flown in from the shadows and snaked its way down his throat. The creature wedged itself into his stomach, driving a spike of hunger deep inside him. With agonizing force, he was yanked awake by the pain, as he doubled over and vomited streams of blood across his bedroom floor. His heart thudded against his chest like a drumbeat, as terror and fear brought a burning to his throat.

Gasping for air, he clawed his way to his feet and stumbled into the kitchen like a man possessed. With shaking hands, he yanked open the refrigerator door so hard it nearly fell off its hinges, and without even bothering to look inside, he grabbed anything in sight and shoved it into his gaping maw: spoiled yogurt, moldy lunch meat, raw eggs with their shells still intact, slimy spinach, and chunks of butter that only made his stomach churn harder. His desperate hunger knew no bounds as he devoured everything within reach.

For a few moments, after stuffing himself to the edge of bursting, he believed he was alright. But then suddenly, his nausea flared anew, and he stumbled blindly towards the bathroom. Desperately, he splashed his face with handfuls of icy water in a vain attempt to soothe the fire in his gut. When he looked up into the mirror, a chill ran through him as he saw that his skin had grown taut and drawn across his face. Frantically pulling off his shirt, he stared at his chest in horror—his ribs were jutting out, transforming him into an animated skeleton before his very eyes.

He felt the rumble in his stomach once more and watched in horror as his skin stretched even tighter around his body. Eyes bulging with madness, he howled in agony and fell to the floor as his body began to convulse violently, writhing in seizure-like spasms as decay coursed through his veins.

After a long time, the seizures stopped and Uri lay on the floor motionless, his eyes now protruding from something barely more than a skull covered with flesh and no muscle in between.

Driven now by nothing more than a primal need for sustenance, the young man slowly pulled himself up and stumbled back to the kitchen, forgetting that he had already devoured its contents earlier. Weakly, he shuffled his way toward the front door and exited out into the street in search of anything that might drive back the hunger.

He would've been astonished to see so many people already roaming the street in the same condition as he, had his mind still worked that way. Instead, now he walked and moved like an automaton, searching for one thing, and one thing only: nourishment.

More than a few of the walking flesh-covered skeletons were engaged in fights with each other, trying desperately to take a bite out of the other's flesh, somehow thinking that cannibalism would save them.

***

Famine sneered before he took a deep breath and opened his mouth wide. An endless swarm of locusts flew from his mouth and converged on the skeletal crowd. Within minutes, the scavenger insects had stripped the flesh from everything in their paths, leaving behind a litter of bones covering the city streets.

Only Uri remained, still possessed by the gnawing hunger that had driven him from his home. Famine shuffled over to him and jammed his finger through the man's belly button. A second later, he pulled a long, wriggling black worm from his stomach. Uri howled in pain as he pulled and pulled until the creature—measuring nearly five feet long—lay writhing on the ground. It gave a soft, high-pitched squeal before it disintegrated into a pool of black ooze.

As Uri stumbled to the ground, the hunger no longer consuming him, Famine said, "Count yourself lucky. The hunger you felt is nothing compared to the hunger my Master has for that which is rightfully his."

Chapter 33

The Gaza Strip.

Although not very large geographically, it is one of the densest populated areas on the Earth. For most of the twentieth century, it had been a major source of political unrest and controversy for the Middle East. Recently, however, Israel had withdrawn its military force from the area, hoping to work toward a peaceful future. Tonight, those hopes would be destroyed.

Death smiled. All those souls crammed together in one tiny, little corner of the globe, just waiting to be ripped apart!

The night sky crackled with electricity and a fierce wind ripped through the countryside as Death raised his arms to the heavens. His booming voice echoed through the land, "Rise, my children!"

From the cracks in the earth, an army of undead warriors emerged. Their clawed hands grabbed at the dirt as they clambered out from their graves. The more recently deceased still had bits of rotting flesh clinging to their bones. In mere moments, a vast horde of monsters was assembled outside Gaza City, ready to reignite the conflict that plagued The Strip in ages past.

The unsuspecting citizens slumbered on, innocently dreaming their happy dreams, blissfully unaware of the horrors that lurked in the shadows of darkness.

***

Miriam kneeled in the fading light of the setting sun, her hands trembling as she ran her fingers across the cover of the photo album. For months since his death, this was her nightly ritual; a chance to re-live all their memories that were captured within its pages and keep them fresh until they could join each other again in the afterlife.

She'd been devastated when he passed, and it had been almost impossible for her not to think about ending her own life so that she could be with him again. But as soon as the thought surfaced, she quickly shook it off, knowing that it wasn't what he would have wanted.

Just as she opened up the first album a low tremor rumbled beneath her feet, causing her heart to hammer against her chest. Weapons testing had become an all-too-common occurrence, yet no matter how many times this happened, each one still struck fear into her soul. Trapped in this war-torn country, conflict was just another part of everyday life.

Miriam continued perusing through her albums, chuckling periodically at one of the many pictures she had of her husband doing something silly—one with a goofy grin on his face as she snapped the photo; another of him wearing a silly outfit with his grandchildren on his lap. She ran her finger softly around the edges of the image, a soft tear welling up in her eye.

Suddenly, she stopped. Something didn't feel right!

She couldn't quite grasp it, but as she sat there, a cold

shiver coursed down her spine. Then she heard the sound—
A chorus of low wails in the distance, like an icy wind
churning through the Mediterranean Sea as it worked its way
toward land.

A series of crashes and explosions moments later sent
Miriam jumping from her chair. Against her better judgment,
she walked to the front window and peered outside. The sky
was a myriad of orange and red dancing to a disastrous beat
as fires raged upward in the distance. Then, she thought she
saw movement down the road. Determined to get a better
view, she went to the front door and cracked it open. She
shouldn't have.

The shadows moved in herky-jerky gaits, accompanied by
cries that nearly stopped her heart from beating. Then the
screams started.

She slammed the door shut and locked it, praying silently
for deliverance. That's when she heard the noise behind her
—a loud clatter from dishes knocked off the table, followed
by wet, sticky footsteps and that same low moan that now
filled the air in all directions. But this was a singular voice.
One that she knew. Tears filled her eyes before she even
turned around.

When she did, she saw him standing there, a shallow
reflection of the man she used to love. She knew he wasn't
human anymore, but had become something dark and vile.
His flesh had rotted from the long months underground, but
not long enough for the worms and maggots to devour him
completely, so that pieces of him flopped to the ground as he
moved. He came at her with hunger and fury in his eyes.

"No, Eitan!" she cried as she slunk to the floor with her
back against the door. The tears were flowing fast and fierce
as she watched her dead husband advance toward her.
"Please, Eitan. Not like this! I don't want this to be my last

memory of you."

But it was too late. A moment later, he was on her, ripping at her feverishly.

She put up no resistance as she died. No matter the monster before her, she still loved him, even unto her death, as she had promised so long ago.

***

Screams echoed through the city as shadows of death danced in the skies above. The hoard descended upon the outlying homes like a plague, turning the streets crimson with blood.

Panic-stricken people raced for safety, only to find certain doom at the hands of the undead. A few brave souls managed to escape, heading south towards Old City and its Great Mosque. But even within the hallowed walls of the sacred ground, they couldn't find solace. The doors split and splintered as the monsters burst inside, relentless and unyielding as their numbers seemed to swell infinitely. Those left alive tried desperately to fight back, but their efforts were futile, for every monster they killed, a hundred more were there to take its place.

By the time dawn approached, only one person remained alive within the city. Inside the Porphyrus Church, an elderly blind woman sat huddled in the corner of a small room located deep in the basement, calling feebly for help.

Her body stiffened as she felt the icy hand of Death caressing its bony fingers across her cheek. Though blind, she knew the nature of the monster that stood before her. Summoning her last ounce of will, she spat in the demon's face—her ultimate act of defiance.

Death's skeletal claw shot up and grabbed the woman by

her throat. Lifting her from the ground, he held her mouth close to his and inhaled deeply. The woman began to spasm as her life was extracted from her. A second later, her body had shriveled into a leathery mass. Her head exploded against the wall as Death threw her wasted body from him.

Chapter 34

An ear-splitting roar erupted from Leviathan as he spotted the looming cruise ship in the Mediterranean Sea. "Yehodi!"

The misshapen head of the priest on his chest moved and twitched. It turned a little to the right, a little to the left, then burst from Leviathan's chest, transforming into an ethereal figure that streaked toward the ship. Its ghostly hair whipped through the air like embers of a roaring fire, lighting up the night sky.

The specter ripped through the hull of the boat with a deafening force, sending shock-waves through its engine room. Shouts of terror were drowned out by a thunderous bang as sparks rained down on the horrified workers. With one final shrieking sound, the engines died and silence fell over the vessel.

***

Nancy stared at the ring on her finger and tears started to well up in her eyes. She had no idea how she was supposed to feel, and if the first night of their honeymoon was anything to go by, she might never comprehend it.

When Ted popped his head into the bathroom, Nancy jolted out of her trance. "You better get ready or we're going to be late for dinner," he said.

Nancy embraced him tightly and said, "I'd rather just stay here and savor this moment."

Ted kissed her softly on the forehead as she clung onto him. "As wonderful as that sounds, it's not every day you get invited to have dinner with the captain."

She put on an exaggerated, pouty face. "Okay, okay, you win. Give me fifteen minutes and I'll be ready!"

"You have ten," Ted replied with a smirk before retreating from the room.

And like clockwork, fifteen minutes later Nancy walked back into the bedroom looking more beautiful than ever—even more than when they had become husband and wife earlier that day. She was dressed in a slender red dress, with matching heels and a pearl necklace. But the most exquisite part of her attire was the ring on her finger. It told the world that she was his.

"Wow!" he said. "I'm going to have a hell of a time keeping the guys away from you tonight!"

Nancy chuckled, "We could always stay here like I suggested earlier?"

"Okay, Mrs. Anderson. That's enough jokes for one night."

She made her pretend pouty face again as he led her from the cabin. "I'm still not quite used to it," she said.

"Used to what?"

"Being called Mrs. Anderson."

"I can call you something else, if you'd like," Ted replied with a smirk.

"We can still go back to our room and you can call me anything you want."

Ted raised an eyebrow and she knew she'd better not push

the issue further. It's not that she didn't want to enjoy a nice dinner with the captain. She just didn't enjoy crowds very much. Or people in general. The world had become an ugly place, with too many ugly people in it, so she tried to avoid them as much as possible for her own peace of mind.

They made their way down the hallway until they came to a set of stairs that lead them from the Emerald Deck down to the Promenade Deck, where the captain was, hopefully, waiting for them to join him.

Luckily, they arrived just seconds after the captain had taken his seat at the head of the table himself. Tall, dark, and distinguished, Captain Rivera was nearly the spitting image of Ricardo Montalban, which was appropriate because to Nancy and Ted, they felt like they were very much on Fantasy Island. The others in attendance were a mixture of business people and entertainers, some young, some old, and all already fallen under the influence of alcohol.

The captain stood back up as the couple approached the table. "Ah, the bride and groom have arrived! I trust you find the honeymoon suite to your liking?"

Nancy replied, "It's wonderful! The underwater view is breathtaking!"

"I'm glad you like it!"

He raised his glass to the newlywed couple. "I propose a toast. To the Andersons! May they enjoy long life and happiness together!"

A chorus of cheers circled the table.

Then a loud screech suddenly sounded through the ship as the metal giant lurched for a moment before it came to a complete stop. A few of the guests grew uneasy, but most simply paused for a second before continuing with their various activities.

A worried look came over Captain Rivera as he excused

himself from the table and hurried toward the elevator at the back of the dining area.

Nancy clenched Ted's hand tightly as a look of fear crept over her face.

"Everything's okay," he tried to assure her. "It's probably just some sort of mechanical malfunction. I'm sure they'll have it fixed in no time."

"I hope so. I'm getting freaked out here."

A moment later, the electricity went out, throwing them into darkness. Panic followed as screams rose from the frightened passengers.

Then the ship turned, slowly at first, then faster and faster. The force threw the passengers to the floor, where they found themselves the targets of falling furniture and flying debris. Wine bottles became glass missiles; eating utensils dangerous weapons; even the décor proved deadly as one man was impaled by the tip of a large swordfish that had hung on the wall only minutes before.

Ted lay on the floor, bleeding from a cut on the top of his head where it had struck the table when he fell. A few feet away, Nancy cried uncontrollably. He reached out to her, trying to grab her hand as she pleaded desperately. Then the power of the spin increased a hundredfold, and they were both pulled in opposite directions by the centrifugal force to the outside walls of the ship. That was the last image both of them had before they died.

***

Once the vessel was rendered powerless, drifting through the water like a ghost ship, Leviathan soared downward until he was only a couple hundred yards above the crippled ship and beat his wings feverishly. As the wind bore down on the ship, he flew in a tight circle directly above, causing the sea to spin and churn. A moment later, a colossal funnel of water shot up, carrying the ship and its contents high into the air. He increased his velocity around the watery vortex until a loud creaking sound permeated through the air as the metal structure of the ship moaned and groaned under the force. Then the weaker force gave way to the stronger, and the ship was wrenched in two.

Then, Leviathan stopped suddenly, and the tempest disappeared, sending the fragmented pieces of the ship crashing back into the sea. Those that hadn't perished during the initial attack quickly found themselves sinking in a watery grave.

Chapter 35

Belial stood tall above the abyss, looking upon the depths of its darkness with an air of power and authority. With a single bound, he was gone, swallowed by the night and suddenly reappearing in the confines of the asylum.

The putrid stench of filth and despair filled his lungs as he marched down the hall like a conqueror. He allowed himself to savor every pungent odor marking this place as his own—the walls reeking of urine and feces, the floor stained with forgotten histories—a reminder that home must be reclaimed.

With a mighty roar, Belial threw open the doors to the recreation room, sending his loyal subjects into tumultuous quivering ecstasy. They may have been deformed creatures, but their loyalty was absolute and they honored their master with enthusiasm. He smiled with pride at their grotesque beauty, a cruel smirk tugging at his lips. His subjects writhed about before him like hideous beasts. Despite their grotesque exterior, they were truly beautiful creatures.

"Patience, my children," he said. "It's almost time. As the death toll rises, man's faith will falter. Then I will reveal my plan to those that guard the gates, portraying Lucifer as the traitor he is. After we help push him back into the pit where he belongs, they will have no choice but to let us in."

Another round of howls rose from his broken children. And he couldn't be happier.

He was just about to call for Nazur when the little man appeared next to him.

"Do you have any updates, Nazur?" Belial asked.

Nazur held his clipboard up close to his face and flipped through several pages. "Yes, Master, I do, indeed. Everything seems to be going perfectly!"

He scribbled on one page with a black pen. "War destroyed Bethlehem easily, reducing the Nativity Scene to rubble, and annihilating the Church of St. Catherine."

Belial nodded, "That's a good start."

Nazur flipped to the next page, "Famine, although not as graceful as War, but effective nonetheless, took out most of Nazareth. He did this thing with a worm that he pulled from a guy's stomach that was quite the spectacle!"

"That sounds quite gruesome," Belial said. "I like it!"

Another page, and after scribbling more notes, Nazur said, "Pestilence brought her plague down on Jerusalem with fury. Apparently, when you sever her tail, it mutates and morphs into living creatures. We need to remember that for future reference. It might come in handy again sometime."

"Duly noted," Belial replied.

Nazur flipped to the last page, read it for a few seconds, and lowered his clipboard to his side. "And Death threw Gaza City into turmoil. Unrest is the law of the land once more." Then, as an afterthought, he added, "Even Leviathan got into the act, destroying a cruise ship in the Mediterranean; ripped it in half like a piece of wet clay."

Belial replied with a smile, "Good. How is the world reacting to news of the destruction? Do they realize that a war is going on?"

"Unfortunately, I'm afraid that the news agencies aren't moving as swiftly as we'd like, Master. But keep in mind that these attacks happened at night. Once the sun rises, they'll see the extent of the horror and report accordingly."

Belial frowned. He wanted the world to cower in fear, believing the prophecies were coming to pass. Whether they were real, didn't matter to him. He just needed them to think they were.

Belial asked, "Did you repair the equipment like I asked?"

"Yes, Master."

"Good."

Nazur followed Belial down the hallway until they made a series of turns that brought them back to the main control room.

When Belial looked at the woman who now occupied the chair, he frowned in disappointment. The woman was Jane Toppin, aka "Jolly Jane". She was one of his favorites, an individual completely misunderstood for her contribution to the medical field in her attempt to aid those suffering and alone. While most considered her helping those many souls cross over acts of murder, Belial considered them acts of kindness—she was merely helping those who couldn't help themselves.

"Not Jane!" he said. "Why her?"

Nazur replied, "Because of the time constraints that we're under, I had to find someone strong enough quickly."

"What happened to Elizabeth?"

Nazur pointed to the opposite corner of the room, where Elizabeth Bathory's body lay slumped in the corner. "She was all used up. I couldn't get enough juice from her to power the equipment again."

"Damn! I thought she'd last a lot longer than this. Oh well, let's get started."

Nazur dragged two metal buckets over and placed each one directly beneath the arms of the chair. Then, after attaching a large clamp to them that resembled jumper cables connecting the buckets to the cable in the back, he ran a sharp knife down each arm so that blood flowed into the buckets.

He looked at Belial. "Ready, Master?"

Belial smiled and replied, "Ready!"

Nazur flipped a large switch on the wall behind the chair and a surge of electricity flowed through the chair, causing "Jolly Jane" to shake and tremble violently. Her eyes opened wide, bugging out of their sockets. Even with the ball-gag in her mouth, a muffled cry still echoed through the room.

After a second, the monitors on the wall came to life as white static covered their screens and hissing issued from their speakers.

Belial picked up a large silver spoon from the table next to him and walked over to the chair, where Jane had begun to smolder from the electricity coursing through her. He patted her on the cheek lightly. "I want you to understand, dear, just how much I appreciate everything you've done, and will now continue to do so for a long time."

Then he stuck the edge of the spoon into the corner of her left eye, prying it from behind until it came out with a 'pop'. He repeated the process on the right eye, and then took the bloody orbs back to the table, where he placed them into a small metal box filled with a black gel that was attached directly to the bank of monitors by another series of wires. Instantly, a series of images sprang onto the screens, each one depicting his Horsemen as they carried out their attacks.

He watched each episode hungrily, relishing in their destruction. Everything was playing out perfectly! He would be going home soon.

Chapter 36

Belial gazed eagerly into the monitors, watching the first moments of his war going exactly as planned. Soon, the chains that bound him to this accursed realm would be shattered, and he would be free to go home. One eternity in this forsaken place was enough. He would not endure another.

Nazur's report of the world above's slow reaction to the carnage was a little disappointing, though. He needed to up the stakes!

"Excuse me," he said to Nazur as he turned to leave. "I'll be back in a minute."

"Do you want me to keep the power on?" Nazur asked.

"Yes. I won't be gone long."

He left the room and walked eagerly down the hall. He had an idea that was sure to get the media's attention!

After a couple of turns, he came to another door, this one locked. After retrieving the key from his pocket, he opened it to reveal a set of stairs descending downward into a black abyss.

As Belial stepped into the room at the end of the stairs, a chill of excitement ran up his spine as he thought about his next move. His reverie was interrupted almost immediately, however. In the empty corner stood a small couch shrouded in shadows, and before it, a crackling fireplace that seemed to bring to life the sinister figure lying on the couch. He recognized Jezebeth immediately, her tall form shimmering in and out of reality.

"Jezebeth! What in the hell are you doing here?" Belial spat.

She smiled wickedly, her dark hair falling past her shoulders like a veil of midnight. "Thanks to our friend Solomon," she said with an evil glint in her eyes, "I can't be here physically right now."

Solomon! A bitter taste rose in Belial's throat.

"Now, don't go getting distracted, sweet cheeks," Jezebeth said, "Or you're going to fuck everything up."

Belial's face twisted with contempt as he glared at Jezebeth. She was a dangerous and unpredictable menace, one that he had no desire to deal with at the moment. He could feel his limbs quivering with rage, his fists balling up in anger. His patience for her was wearing thin quickly. "What is it you want, Jezebeth?" he asked.

"I just wanted to let you know Azazel knows what you're up to. And he's...shall we say...concerned?"

"What does Azazel have to do with anything? He's trapped, and will stay trapped for eternity."

Jezebeth laughed, "Eternity? Yeah, right! He's just waiting for his time. And that time is coming soon. And believe me, he remembers how you betrayed him to Solomon."

"I'd prefer you not say that name again."

"Oh, so he's going to be he-who-must-not-be-named now?"

"Enough games, Jezebeth!"

"Okay, okay. Azazel would just as soon have you out of

the picture, so you don't interfere with him down the road. So, he wants to see you succeed. He's just not sure you will."

Belial chuckled, "What does he know?"

"His power rivals yours, Belial. Remember that. And he feels like your plan lacks a certain finishing point—a knock-out punch—if you will."

"And what would he propose?"

"If you were to break the seal, he and the other demons Solomon imprisoned would gladly help you with your little plan. Then you'd be free to go back home. Although, why you'd want to go back there is anybody's guess?"

"You'd never understand. And in answer to your proposal, even if I knew where Solomon hid the seal, I'd rather do this on my own than be indebted to Azazel and the others."

"Suit yourself. Don't say I didn't warn you. But if Azazel knows what your plan is, surely Lucifer does, too."

Then Jezebeth disappeared, leaving Belial standing there with a foul taste in his mouth. After a moment, he waked toward the blazing fireplace and stepped into it.

He appeared a second later, standing before Leviathan and the Horsemen atop the cliffs surrounding Navagio Beach, also known as Smugglers Cove.

"Your destruction has been quite impressive so far, my children!" he said. "We need one more push to bring this world to its knees. Vatican City—the Holy See. Bring the entire place crumbling to the ground. Then, drag the body of the Pope out into the open for all to see. His death will throw the Catholic Church into turmoil. Then the entire world will finally believe that God is truly dead."

Chapter 37

A young woman rushed into the room and whispered in Gabriel's ear before running back down the corridor toward the main room.

"Excuse us for a moment, please," Gabriel said to Michael before he and the other Archangels walked a short distance away and discussed the situation. Michael watched as the conversation became animated, with Azrael exhibiting his opinions much more openly than the others.

A minute later, Gabriel walked back to Michael with a sense of urgency to his step. "There's been a change of plans. A recent development has forced us to speed up our original plan and send you back much sooner than expected."

"But I thought my body wasn't ready?" Michael asked. "Didn't you say that if I went back down now, I'd die again? And this time it would be permanent?"

"We've dispatched a special group of angels to assist you in the healing process even as we speak. Hopefully, they'll be able to complete their assignment quickly."

"I really don't like the 'hopefully' part of that statement," Michael said.

He looked down and saw a score of angels circling his

body in one continuous motion, each one glowing brightly as it delivered its healing touch.

As Michael stood watching the events in the tower below, Azrael addressed his battalion of angels, "The time has come...much sooner than expected. Belial moves now to destroy the faith of man. That we cannot allow. You must deter Leviathan and the Horsemen long enough to allow Michael's body to heal. Then he and the Chosen Ones will destroy the abominations."

Azrael waved his sword through the air, and the angels sped away.

Michael looked at Gabriel, "Time's running out, isn't it?"

"Yes," replied the Archangel. "But hope is not yet lost."

***

The morning air was saturated with the heady aroma of lilacs, which drew Mary to a grassy field. As she skipped across the dew-laden blades of grass, butterflies fluttered around her, iridescent wings unfurling in an ethereal waltz. The crisp chirps of robins and sparrows filled the sky, a soundtrack that accompanied the steady climb of the sun towards its zenith.

A small clearing opened up before her, where she saw a solitary morning-dove sitting among a patch of wildflowers, cooing softly for its lost soul mate. She approached the bird slowly, speaking gently as she drew near. "What's the matter, little fella? Are you lost?"

A soft voice spoke up behind her, "Among all of earth's creatures, the morning dove is one of the most loyal. Once it finds a mate, it will stay with that mate for life. They are wholly and completely dedicated to each other."

Startled, Mary turned around to find Father Thomas

standing there. "You are like that dove, Mary. Even during the darkest of times, you knew deep down inside your heart that the love Michael and you shared was complete. Now you wait for your mate to return to you, but he is not here."

"I know," Mary replied softly. "I miss him so much. How do I find him?"

"His body waits for you now, but soon his spirit will enter a terrible struggle. You must be there to help him in this battle. Climb the highest tower at St. Anthony's. There you will find him."

Suddenly, everything around Mary disappeared into blackness. She vaguely felt the hard surface of her bedroom floor beneath her as she teetered on the border between dreamland and the waking world.

The voice echoing in her head snapped her fully to consciousness, *Hurry Mary, Michael needs you!*

Her eyes shot open.

Hesitantly, she wiggled her fingers; then her toes. When she felt the tingling in her extremities, she issued a sigh of relief. She vividly recalled the desperate feelings while being paralyzed. She never wanted to feel that way again!

She jumped up and ran out of her apartment, not even stopping to change from her pajamas. The only thing on her mind was Michael.

In her bare feet, she bounded down the steps to the landing and ran out the door. Debris and wreckage lined the area from the storm that had passed through, and a deep frown crossed her face when she saw the twisted remains of her car buried under the trunk of a giant uprooted tree.

Quickly, she bound down the steps and winced in pain as her foot landed on a jagged rock. But the pain was nothing compared to the urgency that controlled her as she ran, bloody footprints following her on the pavement.

Mary stumbled to a halt, her feet skidding against the ground as she saw the gaping abyss that stretched in front of St. Anthony's Church. Flames danced around its edges and the ruins of the building's massive door lay in smoldering pieces at her feet. But all Mary could see in her mind was Michael's body lying at death's doorstep.

Her legs pumped beneath her as she raced up the steps, dodging shards of wood and wreckage that was scattered like shrapnel from a bomb. As she ran through the sanctuary, she clung to the image of the giant crucifix that hung behind the altar as if it were her only lifeline. Taking two steps at a time, Mary scaled the stairs toward the top of the tower, her heart heavy with dread.

The door to the tower stood blackened and charred from the fire that had raged there just a short time ago. With a trembling hand, she grabbed hold of the handle and was met with an eerie silence when it creaked open on its own.

A sob escaped Mary's throat when she saw Michael's body laid out upon the cot. She fell to her knees beside him, pressing her face into his motionless chest as tears streamed down her cheeks. Wracked with guilt, all Mary could whisper between sobs was, "I'm sorry."

***

Gabriel looked at Michael, "It's time."

He touched Michaels's forehead, "God be with you."

Suddenly, Michael felt like he was caught in a giant vacuum being pulled back toward his body.

***

A brilliant white light engulfed Michael, as if a million stars

213

had converged to bring him back to life. His body shuddered as a deafening roar burst from his lungs when his spirit reentered. He blinked back the tears that had formed from the intensity of the light. As the light subsided, Mary's face slowly came into view and every ounce of Michael's being settled peacefully as he looked at her.

Michael sat up and held Mary tight. "Oh, Mary," he cried, "I'm so sorry...for everything."

He barely finished his sentence when a searing pain tore through his stomach. He gasped and clutched his abdomen as he collapsed on the floor, his body convulsing in spasms. He looked up at her, his eyes wide with fear as he felt the poison coursing through his veins, burning him from the inside. "Help me," he pleaded hoarsely.

Mary held his head in her hands, feeling his life slip away. She wanted to break down and cry, but she knew he needed her to be strong. "Fight it, Michael!" she urged. "Fight it like you've never fought before!"

When his eyes rolled back into his head, panic set in. *You can't die now, not when you're so close!*

"Don't you quit on me, Michael!" Mary pleaded. "Heaven and Earth need you...I need you."

Those last three words did the trick.

Michael weakly rose to his knees and vomited the last of the poison from his body onto the tower floor. As his strength slowly returned, he looked up at Mary and smiled. He was alive again, and it was all because of her.

Chapter 38

Belial smiled like a young stud on prom night as he walked back into the control room and took his seat again in front of the monitors. "Now, where were we?" he said to Nazur. "Ah, yes...the total annihilation of Vatican City! This should be fun!"

He turned to Nazur. "Give it a little more juice, Nazur. I don't want to risk losing reception."

Nazur took his knife out and cut into Jane's flesh once more, this time starting up at the top of her shoulder and dragging the blade down to her wrist. Once he had repeated this process on the other arm, he went over to a small equipment stand near the back of the chair that held an apparatus resembling an amplifier. He turned a couple of the dials to adjust the reception, causing Jane to jump and twitch even more. "How's that?" he asked.

"Perfect!" Belial replied. He inched his chair closer to the table, resembling a child eager to watch his favorite cartoon on Saturday morning.

***

Leviathan laughed when he saw the group of angels

suddenly surrounding them. "This should be fun!" he said with a wicked sneer.

The Horsemen quickly shot out like the wind in four different directions and attacked with savage abandon. The angels never had a chance.

War swung his mighty ax hard and wide, destroying a barrage of angels with one blow. Those he missed the first time were sliced in two as he brought his weapon back around.

In the opposite direction, the black-robed figure of Death dove from his nightmare and flew through the sky like a wraith. His form changed to a misty substance as he charged forward. A second later, a loud shriek issued from the nearest angel as Death's shadow flew through its chest and burst out its back. Then the angel's lifeless body fell toward the earth. A flurry of dead angels followed, as Death continued his deadly trajectory.

Not to be outdone, Pestilence reared her serpent-head back and let fly a stream of acid. The smell of charred feathers filled the airy battlefield, followed by the tortured screams of angels spiraling downward to join their fallen comrades as their wings melted like wax on a burning candle.

Famine raced to finish the massacre. His nightmare sped around the perimeter at blinding speed, bellowing monstrous fireballs at the remaining opposition, sending them to join their fallen brethren.

As the flames engulfed and incinerated them, Leviathan smiled. The demon looked up defiantly, "Is that the best you can do?"

***

Belial could hardly contain himself as he watched his

warriors lay waste to the opposition. With every drop of angelic blood spilled, his plan was a step closer to success. His face beamed with anticipation as the main event was about to start!

He rushed back toward the recreation room and threw the doors open once again, his voice filled with excitement as he addressed the crowd, "The time has come, my children. Go now and destroy everything in your path. Make Heaven bleed. And remember to tell them that Lucifer sent you!"

A chorus of demonic cries echoed through the asylum as each inmate underwent a traumatic metamorphosis. Wings and claws, horns and fangs, sprouted from their twisted bodies, transforming them into fearsome soldiers. A fiery portal opened in the back wall of the room, through which they flew eagerly, loud, demonic cries echoing down the asylum walls as they left.

A series of loud, metallic clicks followed this, as the doors to the maximum-security chambers were opened—the rooms reserved for the blackest of souls. Inside lived the vilest people to ever walk the earth—Jack the Ripper, Death's silent assassin; Lizzy Borden, whose unbridled fury with an ax would give War a run for his money; H. H. Holmes, who had killed without remorse; their names imparted fear while they were still alive, carried on whispers to frighten young children who didn't do as they were told. Now, they would instill that same fear in the afterlife as they led the charge against Heaven and all that was righteous.

Apart from his Horsemen, his 'Dream Team' would be the most fearsome group ever assembled. No longer bound by the limitations of the human body, they were poised to unleash their devastation on an epic scale. How could the angels possibly hope to stand against such unfettered evil?

This would all but assure his victory!

Chapter 39

Azrael's heart felt like a stone in his chest. He had never imagined such horror. His grief grew with each drop of angelic blood that stained the ground.

He turned to his remaining soldiers, his eyes blazing with fury and pain. "Go now and avenge those that have fallen!" he roared.

This time, a legion of angels soared to confront the behemoths. Azrael prayed their sheer numbers could stall the beasts long enough for Michael and the Chosen Ones to join the battle. Then they would have a chance to turn the tide.

***

When Michael saw the destruction outside the church, a wave of sadness coursed through him, for he knew firsthand that this was only a fraction of the devastation that the Horsemen had already caused.

As Mary and him passed through the doorway into the open air, they saw the four Chosen One's standing there, waiting with hardened eyes and firm resolve chiseled on their faces.

"I'm glad to see that you survived the accelerated healing process," Gabriel said as he appeared beside them. "We were all quite concerned."

"I almost didn't," Michael said as he looked at Mary. "It was Mary who got me through it. Without her, I wouldn't have had the strength to fight."

"Heaven is forever in your debt," Gabriel said as he bowed toward Mary. Then his gaze shifted back to Michael.

"Unfortunately, we don't have time to dwell on your victory. As we speak, the angels are fighting the Horsemen high above Rome. They must not enter Vatican City at all cost!"

Michael looked at Mary sadly, "I love you with all my heart."

Mary responded by grabbing him and holding him tightly. Then she did the hardest thing she'd ever done; what she knew she had to do. She let him go.

"I know," she said through teary eyes. "And now you need to make me a promise."

"What's that?"

"That you'll send those bastards back into Hell where they fucking belong."

Michael smiled for a second before his face became serious, "I promise."

Gabriel interjected, "It's time to go, Michael."

"There's one tiny problem," Michael said. "I can't fly."

"Press the button in the center of your breastplate," Gabriel said.

Michael hadn't noticed the golden jewel at first, thinking it was just an ornate part of his suit. When he pressed it, a pair of wings sprang from his back. He looked at Gabriel in surprise.

Gabriel said, "That should get the job done."

The Chosen Ones followed suit, and a second later, they were ready for battle.

Then the man who was once a loser and a junkie, with no hope for redemption, turned and walked away from Mary with the weight of the universe on his shoulders. But he didn't bend or break under this pressure. He held his head up high as he steeled himself for the battle to come. Then he launched himself into the air.

Chapter 40

As Azrael stood firm with the rest of his army, the small legion that always stood guard on the hills surrounding the two-hundred-foot jasper walls that protected the City of God, he heard the screeching cries of the approaching enemy before he saw them. And when they came into view, they were horrifying beyond belief. These weren't Lucifer's demons, they were something far more terrible; unadulterated evil in its purest form, and they ravaged through the diminished forces of Heaven with unbridled fury. He had expected some form of attack on the main front, but nothing like this!

As the front line bent under the relentless brutality, Azrael urged his troops on with a mighty cry, "Do not surrender to their evil! Fight to protect all that is righteous and holy!"

In response to his cry, the angels pushed the first wave of demons back, keeping the gates of Heaven secure...for now. Filled with renewed determination, the angels met the demon's ferocity equally. Howls of agony rose from the creatures as the angel's weapons found their mark. The battle seemed won as the demons turned and fled back, away from the front-line.

It was just the beginning.

The demons regrouped and advanced a second time, led by the Souls of the Damned. Lizzy Borden carved a path of carnage through the defenders as she swung her twin axes with the ferocity of a maniac, staining her blades with the blood of countless angels. Jack the Ripper swooped down upon his unsuspecting foes, slithering in and out among them like a shadow, his dagger striking silently with deadly accuracy repeatedly. H. H. Holmes, dressed in a gas mask with a flamethrower strapped to his back, sprayed a toxic cloud of gas on the angels before lighting them on fire. Their screams echoed throughout all of Heaven as they died.

Azrael called to a handful of angels nearby, "Go to the battle below and tell them that Heaven is under attack! Everyone needs to fall back now!"

Like a tidal wave brought on by a tsunami, the demons crashed into the waiting forces. Azrael took up his sword and met the savage attacks of Lizzy. Gabriel joined the fray and stood his ground firmly while locked in battle against The Ripper. Holmes, however, went unchecked.

Behind them, the Archangel Michael waited with a small band of angels as the last defense outside Heaven's Gates. Their only hope was to hold out for reinforcements to return.

Then time ran out.

For a moment, Azrael met Lizzy's attack equally. But her fury wore him down. She was relentless, pounding at him without mercy. And then the unthinkable happened. As he parried one of her thrusts away, she brought her other ax up in a wide arc that caught him in the chest and carried upward, splitting his skull in two.

Likewise, Gabriel was locked in mortal combat with The Ripper, who moved like a wraith, avoiding every attack that the Archangel could muster. And when Gabriel's blade found the demon's body, it passed through it like it was mist, causing virtually no harm. Not so with The Ripper. His dagger found Gabriel's flesh repeatedly, slicing long paths where the blood flowed freely. Finally, Gabriel fell to his knees and joined his brother in death.

Raphael didn't have time to mourn, however, as he rushed in to meet Holmes' attack, who was swinging his flamethrower back and forth like a madman, spraying his poison into the air. The smell of charred flesh was overpowering as countless angels fell to his unholy flame. Just as Raphael thought he had stopped far enough away from the range of the spray; a small drop caught the tip of his wing. That was all it took for the flames to ignite.

A loud screamed erupted from the Archangel Michael as he watched his brothers fall. It took every ounce of reserve for him to resist the urge to rush forward and avenge their deaths. But he knew that if he did that, the Gates of Heaven would be vulnerable.

***

Belial rushed back to the control room to watch his war play out. He needed his plan to succeed. He needed Lucifer to take the fall. And he needed to go back home.

As he watched his hoard tear through the angels, a smile spread across his face. Then, as his dream team ravaged through the Archangels, he could hardly contain his glee. He was so close to victory that he could taste it.

Then it all came crashing down.

The legion of angels returned, swooping in behind the demon hoard, and converged on them. As the battle continued to unfold, a foul taste was brewing in Belial's mouth. The angels were winning! That was impossible! He had practically handed Heaven over to them, weak and ripe for the slaughter. And yet, somehow, they had managed to display their complete and utter incompetence.

He yelled at the screens like a sports fan screaming at his television after a pitcher had fucked up and given up the game-winning home run. Finally, he stood up and threw his chair at the monitors, sending a shower of sparks through the air as they shattered. That sent a backlash of power back to Jane, who twitched again for a few seconds and then went limp.

He turned to Nazur, "I guess if I want something done right, I'll have to do it myself."

Nazur didn't reply, making himself look busy as he flipped aimlessly through his clipboard.

Belial walked back down toward his private room, fuming the entire way, and then vanished into the fireplace once more.

Chapter 41

As soon as Tresham tried to grab hold of the demon, he realized his mistake. The beast swung around faster than expected and snatched his arm with an unbreakable grip. A cry erupted from the angel as Leviathan grabbed his other arm and pulled until an echo of loud snaps reverberated through the air. Like a downed aircraft, Tresham spiraled to the ground far below.

Meanwhile, the Horsemen were not enjoying the same level of success. Although still not a match in terms of raw power, the angels slowed the monsters down with their sheer numbers alone.

A small group of angels suddenly appeared near the outer fringes of the front line and circled the battlefield, shouting above the clamor, "Fall back, everyone! Heaven is under attack!"

Leviathan and the Horsemen suddenly found the path to the Holy See completely unimpeded. Immediately, they sped downward. The ground shook as Leviathan landed in the middle of St. Peter's Square. A wide grin spread across his twisted face as he saw the bodies of fallen angels littering the courtyard.

The crowd shrank back in terror at the sight of the demons —all, except for one. Dressed in his flowing white robes, the Pope stood defiantly near the entrance to The Sistine Chapel. Even though his body had withered throughout the ages, his spirit was unmovable and his faith unshaken.

Leviathan leaped across the courtyard and landed inches away from the Holy Man. The impact sent another tremor rolling through the earth. Yet still, the Pope remained undaunted.

"You would do well to bow before me, Pontiff," Leviathan bellowed.

"I serve only one master, you abomination of evil. I will bow before no other."

"Then, little man, it is time for you to die!"

Leviathan grabbed the Pope by the throat and lifted him high into the air.

"Put him down, Leviathan!"

The demon spun around to face Michael. The Four Horsemen immediately moved to form a defensive barrier between Michael and Leviathan.

"I was wondering when you'd show up," he said as he patted Yehodi's head like he was a little puppy jutting from his chest. The gnarled face responded with a sequence of silent lip movements, coupled with a flurry of darting eyes. "I hope we haven't caused you any problems along the way?"

Michael replied simply, "I'm here, aren't I?"

Leviathan smiled. "That you are. And I certainly hope you've brought an army with you or this is going to be quick and easy."

"Oh, I think you're gonna be surprised at who I brought."

The Chosen Ones descended swiftly to join Michael.

At first, Leviathan was stunned before he burst into laughter.

"Is that the best Heaven can do—four angel wanna-bees and a junkie loser as their leader?"

"Your arrogance will be your downfall, Leviathan."

Leviathan held the Pope high in the air. "We'll see about that. Let's get this party started right," he said before hurling the holy man across the courtyard like a javelin. The frail body flew through the air, heading for a deadly impact with the massive brick wall that surrounded the area.

Michael raced forward and caught the man inches away from certain death. Gently he laid the Pope on the ground.

"Nice trick," Leviathan said sarcastically, "but it'll take more than parlor tricks to win this war."

"Don't worry," Michael replied, "there's more where that came from."

"Show me," Leviathan said daringly.

"You heard the ugly fuck," Michael said to the Chosen Ones. "Let's show him what we got."

As one, the five of them pointed their swords at the demons. Bolts of lightning shot out, striking each of their targets with a mighty blow. The attack caught the Horsemen off guard and sent them sprawling from their steeds.

Leviathan was the only one left standing.

Immediately, the Chosen Ones soared high into the sky, taking the fight away from the city.

The Horsemen rebounded quickly and charged into the air after them.

***

Belial silently surveyed the battlefield. The beginning to this epic battle had been quite promising, brutal and bloody, savage and gruesome. Just the way he had planned. Now, it had all gone to shit. After being caught off-guard and losing their advantage, his forces seemed to be fighting with much less ferocity than he had hoped; almost with fear in their eyes. Even his Dream Team looked scared and apprehensive. He had hoped that Azrael would not be so quick to react to his initial attack, but apparently their faith in their little band of 'heroes' below was greater than he had thought.

A last-minute idea suddenly flew into Belial's brain. If he played everything right, he could still use this to his advantage. Stretching his arms out wide, he let out a mighty roar as his body grew to ten times its original height and twin, fiery battle-swords appeared in his hands. His appearance resembled Lucifer's true form in every diabolical way. It was time for the ultimate act!

He charged into the melee, swinging his blades with ruthless fury. Two opposing militants nearby met their demise quickly, as their heads were separated from their bodies before they realized he was upon them. Their mouths still twitched as their skulls hit the ground. He smiled as he continued through the battery of angels without mercy, spilling their blood in rivers.

Then Belial saw the Archangel Michael in the distance. He quickly changed back to his normal form and grabbed a blade from the ground. He dragged the blade across his arm, cutting himself deep so the blood flowed freely. Then he staggered toward the group, limping noticeably.

"Thank God, I'm not too late!" he said as he slunk to the ground. "I've come to warn you...Lucifer is trying to...all his idea...tricked me...barely...escaped."

Then he went silent as he sought to sell the lie.

***

Michael was disappointed when Leviathan brushed away his

attack so easily. He called out to those cowering in the courtyard, "Quick, everyone! Get out of here!"

He watched as the crowd scattered frantically for safety. Seconds later, only one person was left standing alongside Michael: Like a captain refusing to abandon his sinking ship, the Holy Man stood unshaken. Michael looked into his eyes and saw a pillar of strength shining through. There was no way this man was going to back down.

Leviathan looked through scornful eyes at Michael, "Okay, now it's my turn!"

Rearing back like a baseball pitcher, he let fly a giant fireball. Michael pointed his sword at the streaking ball of fire. A beam of white energy blasted from the weapon and met the fireball in full force. The collision rocked the courtyard, sending brick and mortar flying in all directions.

However, Michael didn't notice Leviathan sending the demon-head exploding from his chest toward him, catching him completely off-guard. The force of Yehodi slamming into him, sent Michael flying.

With a bone-jarring thud, Michael hit the ground, causing the magical helm to fly from his head and land at the Pope's feet. Leviathan wasted no time.

As Michael rolled to his knees, he suddenly heard Mary crying out to him, "Help me, Michael. Please! I need you!"

"Mary?"

"Why did you leave me like this? Didn't our love mean anything to you?"

Panic started setting in. "Of course, it meant—; I didn't want to—; I had no choice—"

He looked up and saw Mary walking toward him. "Of course, you had a choice, Michael! You always have a choice."

Michael struggled to respond. "But everything will be lost if Belial wins," he pleaded.

"You don't know that for a fact. Heaven might have defeated Belial without you, and we would still be together."

Michael sat there, speechless.

The gap between Michael and the woman he loved with all his heart had shortened to a few yards when he heard the Pope call out to him, "Don't listen to the lies, Michael. Trust your heart. It's not your Love which speaks to you now...it is evil instead."

With the agility of a man half his age, the Holy Man scooped up the helm and charged for Michael. He placed the helm back on his head just as Leviathan closed in on him.

The image of Mary vanished instantly, replaced with Leviathan's grotesque and twisted face. The creature brought his claws around sharply, striking Michael in his side directly under his left arm—the only vulnerable spot where the armor offered no protection. Michael let out a piercing cry as the sharp claws cut deep into his flesh.

Desperately, he brought his sword around and slashed at the beast. The weapon found its mark at the base of the demon's neck. The monster toppled to the ground, writhing for a second before it stopped. Michael fell backward, blood spilling onto the ground from the wound in his side.

"You must release Yehodi's soul," Michael said in a scratchy voice as the Pope rushed over. "That's the only way to destroy the monster."

The Pope made his way to Leviathan's body and looked in horror at the head of Yehodi grafted onto the demon's chest. The mouth moved slowly as if to speak, while his eyes held the look of a frightened child.

Placing his hands firmly upon Yehodi's head, one at each temple, the Holy Man looked toward Heaven and spoke, "Almighty Father, in Your Name I release this soul, to be judged by you and rewarded accordingly."

A bright light shot down from above and engulfed the demon's body. It shook violently before the ghostly essence of Yehodi erupted from its chest. Slowly, it started floating upward until it suddenly stopped and was pulled downward by some unseen force. A moment later, the ground opened up to swallow the lost soul. Yehodi was no more.

Michael said to the Pope through clenched teeth, "I guess he was found wanting."

Chapter 42

Michael looked at the Pope through blurry eyes, the pain coursing through him becoming unbearable. "Thank you, Your Holiness," he said in a raspy voice.

No sooner had the words passed his lips when a terrible coughing fit overtook him.

Worry filled the Holy Man's eyes as he heard the unmistakable sound of blood in Michel's lungs. "Please, try not to talk," he pleaded. "Save your strength. We'll get you to a hospital right away."

Michael reached up and grabbed desperately for the Pope's robes. "No hospital," he croaked. "I have to finish this!"

Seeing the determination in Michael's eyes and hearing the conviction in his voice, the Pope stood back, saying a silent prayer for the fallen hero. "How may I help?" he asked.

Michael replied weakly, "Help me up."

The Pope tried to help Michael to his feet, but he was too weak to stand and slunk back down to the ground.

"You're injured far too badly to continue this fight, young man," the Pope said. "You must seek medical attention or you'll die."

"If I don't end this war, Your Holiness, then a lot of other people will die."

"Then, at least let our physicians try to heal you as best as we can."

Michael conceded, and the Pope scampered away, leaving him alone and teetering on the edge of consciousness. He could feel himself slipping away, and fought hard to keep hold. He would not let everyone down, least of all Mary. He'd done enough of that in the past.

A minute later, the Pope returned with two men running beside him out to the courtyard. As they came to a halt next to Michael, they exchanged nervous glances. The dead body of Leviathan lay only a few yards away, with his severed head just beyond. It was a signal to these men that there were forces at work that they couldn't understand.

The three men worked delicately to remove Michael's armor; each movement bringing a pained cry from his lips. Once they had removed his breastplate, the two physicians shot a grave look toward the Pope and both shook their heads in unison. Blood was pouring profusely from the massive wound, and they knew that nothing in their power would save him short of real medical attention.

The Pope addressed Michael once more, "Are you sure you want to go through with this, Son?"

"I have to, Your Holiness," Michael replied. "I'm tired of running away. I've run away from everything my whole life."

"Then you truly have the heart of a saint! We will do everything we can."

"That's all I ask for."

While the physicians stitched and bandaged his wound shut, the Pope placed his hand on Michael's chest and closed his eyes. The words that came from his lips as he uttered his prayer were foreign to Michael, yet he felt a warm tingle work its way through his body.

After a couple of minutes, Michael slowly tried to stand and found that a good portion of his strength had returned. The pain was still there, but it had been reduced to a dull ache that rested in the background. He knew it was only a matter of time before it surged forward once again in full force.

After the men helped Michael put his armor back on, he bowed toward the Pope. "Thank you, Your Holiness."

The Pope replied, "It is not I who deserves your thanks, young man. But you must know that your healing is only temporary. Another injury such as that may prove fatal."

"Then I'll have to make sure that doesn't happen."

Michael took a deep breath and pressed the button on his breastplate, extending his wings. "Now, Your Holiness, pray as you've never prayed before. The future of all existence hangs in the balance right now."

Then he leaped into the air and soared away, each second bringing the pain inching closer to the surface. *I just need to hold on a little longer,* became his mantra that urged him to keep pushing forward..

Chapter 43

As if they had drawn an invisible line amid the airy battlefield, the combatants stood steadfast for a long moment, sizing up their opponents. On one side, the Four Horsemen growled and roared savagely, trying to intimidate their opponents. The Chosen Ones responded with a look of sheer determination and will. This only infuriated the Horsemen. Immediately, they charged forward, lashing out savagely. The battle had begun.

Almost immediately, the battle splintered off into four separate melees, as each of the Chosen Ones found themselves locked in a fierce conflict with one of the Horsemen.

Peter swooped quickly down to his right, causing War to miss his initial attack by mere inches. The force of the swing and the resulting miss sent the giant reeling off-balance. Peter responded by swinging sharply back around to circle the beast. He brought his fiery sword down and was rewarded with a howl from the Horseman when his blade found its mark and sliced War's hand off. The dismembered appendage still clutched its ax firmly as it fell to the earth below.

Pestilence fumed as she charged toward Ruth. Her cobra hood flared out as her head shot forward, jaws opened wide to reveal her long, sharp fangs. Acid dripped from their tips and burned Ruth's skin as she ducked out of the way barely in time.

Unable to get a clean shot at the demon as she scurried out of the way, Ruth instead fired a blast from her sword that struck the Nightmare carrying the Horseman. The force of the blow caught Pestilence by surprise, sending her flying off her steed. War flew down quickly to grab hold of her with his remaining hand and hoisted her onto the back of his steed.

Meanwhile, Lucas battled toe-to-toe with the decaying form of Famine, while John was locked in combat with the specter of Death. Both fights seemed to be at a standstill, with neither side able to gain an advantage over the other.

A wave of dark energy suddenly rippled through the air, sending the Horsemen into a frenzy. After a moment, each one stopped, and they quickly flew to gather together, extending their arms outward toward each other to form a small circle. They began to chant as a dark cloud appeared to engulf the four demons. Seconds later, the dark mass spun counterclockwise rapidly, sending forks of lightning flying out in all directions. A wave of thunder boomed through the sky that sounded as if the bowels of the Universe were being ripped open.

Then suddenly it stopped.

The Chosen Ones looked at each apprehensively, a hint of fear creeping into their eyes for the first time. When the dark cloud dissipated, a figure more terrifying than anything ever imagined hovered before them. The Four Horsemen were no more. Now they faced Armageddon.

With four powerful arms jutting from its torso, black dragon wings erupting from its back, a long serpentine tail that ended in sharp spikes, razor-sharp claws, and long pointed horns atop its twisted face, the creature sent a terrible chill coursing through the Chosen Ones. But what was the most unsettling were the many eyes that peered out at them from all over its body: two in its normal spot on its face and then one on each cheek, two on its shoulders and its chest, four rotating between the tops and palms of its hands, as did the two in the middle of its wings—it even had eyes covering the tops of its feet and the end of its tail.

They knew immediately that any attempt to surprise the creature would fail miserably, but they had to try. They flew up quickly, trying to surround the massive demon, and attacked it feverishly, their swords striking the beast with a flurry of massive blows.

The great behemoth shrugged off these attacks as if they were nothing, before responding with an offensive charge of its own. In a split second, its four arms shot out simultaneously and struck each of its attackers with a deadly blow. The force of the impact sent the Chosen Ones spiraling out of control toward the earth below.

Chapter 44

Michael flew swiftly toward the fallen warriors. A beam of energy blasted from his sword to engulf each of the four heroes. Instantly, their tumultuous descent stopped.

Glancing up, Michael saw the winged monstrosity roar in anger. Quickly, he turned back to the Chosen Ones. "We only have one chance to defeat this thing. On my cue, release the full power of your weapons toward the center of the beast. Hopefully, the blast will be enough to temporarily blind it and give me the chance I need."

As the creature drew closer, the five of them placed the tips of their swords together and aimed toward their target. Michael waited a few seconds more to ensure that Armageddon was within range. When the time was right, he shouted, "Now!"

The blow struck Armageddon square in its chest. The force of the attack knocked the demon backward, while the resulting explosion created a ball of fire ten times brighter than any sun. Even with their eyes closed, the five heroes reeled in anguish from the intensity.

The roar of pain from Armageddon's mouth told Michael that their initial attack had worked. Now he had the chance he was hoping for.

"Keep blasting away," Michael shouted, "while I fly in to finish him."

The four warriors pelted the beast with blast after blast, while, Michael urged himself forward, toward the giant black stone in the center of Armageddon's chest.

Michael flew higher, closing the distance between him and the demon. Then, his worst fear came true. The stitches pulled through his skin with a loud snap, tearing his flesh open once more. Growing weaker with every passing second, as the blood flowed once more from the gaping wound, Michael knew that he'd only have one shot at this.

Dodging the flailing arms and beating wings, he flew on a wild roller-coaster path that finally brought him to the source of the creature's power.

As Michael reached out to grab hold of the orb embedded in the demon's skin, the blindness in Armageddon's eyes subsided and the demon saw immediately what Michael's intention was.

All four arms grabbed Michael as he placed his hands on the orb. At the same moment that he felt his ribs snap in two and his spine crumble, he ushered his last prayer to the Almighty, "Father, into your hands I offer these souls, to judge accordingly."

A look of bewilderment came over Armageddon as he cried out. An instant later, his wings stopped beating, his arms stopped moving, and his body became rigid. Then Michael fell with the demon to the earth far below.

***

Michael's broken body lay outside the entrance to St. Peter's Basilica. The Pope was bending over him, sadness clinging to his eyes as he issued a last prayer. To his left, some forty yards away, lay the unmoving form of Armageddon. Steam rose from the ground as the beast melted back into the primordial filth from which it had been spawned. They had won this battle. Hopefully, now they would win the war.

The Pope moved away from Michael as the Chosen Ones approached, giving them a moment to mourn. As Ruth bent down and cradled Michael's head in her arms, he opened his eyes one last time. "Thank you," he said weakly. "You have done well."

His gaze shifted upward. "It is finished," he said. Then he died.

Chapter 45

As Belial lay on the ground, he suddenly felt a dark shiver course through him. *Something is wrong!* Then he heard Yehodi's scream in his mind and he knew Leviathan had fallen.

Belial tried to weigh the implications that this recent development would have on his master plan. He was too close to his prize to turn back now. He continued his charade, hoping that his performance was believable enough that the Archangel would take pity on him and let him inside.

Then he felt it again; another wave of emptiness pulled from him that rippled violently through his body, much worse this time than the last. He knew the unthinkable had happened. His Horsemen were no more.

His mind raced! Everything was falling apart even as he saw the finish line directly in front of him. He only had one choice left. He would fight to regain what he had lost, or he would die trying. There was no going back to the same shell of an existence he had lived for the last twenty millennia.

Before he could act, the Archangel said, "Get up, Belial. Your game has gone too far. It's over now."

He opened his eyes and sat up, trying one last time to play

the injured victim. Fierna then stepped from behind the Archangel, her eyes burning with anger. "I tried to warn you, Father, that you'd pay for betraying me! But you insisted on carrying on your foolish little plan."

For the first time in a thousand years, Belial didn't know what to say. He was stunned! He had thought his plan foolproof. Nearly a century of plotting and planning, and it was all for nothing. In the end, everyone had betrayed him. Again.

He looked at Fierna sadly. "You would see me fail like this?"

"Oh, get over yourself, Father!" Fierna said. "Your plan was doomed from the beginning. You were too blinded by your ego to see it, though."

"So, why put your nose in my business, then?"

"Because I like things the way they are, and your little episode was threatening to destroy that. I was hoping if you failed, things could go back to the way they were before, and we could rule together once more. But, unfortunately, that's not a possibility anymore. Plus, a certain Prince of Hell wasn't exactly happy being implicated in your scheme."

Belial sensed his approach before he saw him and stiffened. Everything went silent, like they were in the eye of a hurricane, and then a crack of thunder signaled his arrival. In a move of complete desperation, he called out to his Dream Team—Lizzy, Jack, and Holmes. He knew they wouldn't be able to defeat Lucifer. He just needed them to keep him occupied.

As soon as Lucifer appeared—in grand entry fashion amidst a cloud of smoke and sulfur—the three converged on him in all their fury.

As the three members of his newly formed death squad were keeping Lucifer occupied, Belial drew upon his pent-up rage—rage that had been festering inside him since Father had cast him out. He would not be denied!

"Step aside, Michael," Belial said, "and let me back home where I belong."

The Archangel replied, "Sorry, Belial. You made your decision long ago. Now you have to live with that choice for the rest of eternity."

"We'll see about that," Belial replied as he charged forward, his sword appearing in his hand.

The Archangel dodged the attack easily, and then swung his own sword around, catching Belial with a striking blow across its left forearm.

Belial howled in pain, but his cry quickly exploded into savage wrath as he unleashed a flurry of attacks on the Archangel. Most of these were blocked easily, but for a minuscule second, his blade broke through and slashed Michael across the midsection. This time it was the Archangel's turn to cry out in pain. Belial wasted no time seizing upon this opportunity and moved in for the kill.

He lashed out at the Archangel with a flurry of relentless attacks. with one deadly blow finding its mark. As the Archangel brought his sword up to parry one of those attacks, Belial spun around and drove his blade into his abdomen, cutting him deep. Then, with a powerful thrust upward, he sliced the torso in half. The defeated sentinel fell silent, allowing Belial an unimpeded path to the Gates.

With the look of a crazed barbarian lavishing in the throes of his fallen victim, Belial raced toward the gates. He was just about to reach for the golden handle when a voice stopped him cold, "Not so fast, Belial!"

Belial turned around, irritated. He recognized the voice immediately as the source of all his anguish and frustration. *Why won't this piss-ant fuck just die already?* He thought bitterly.

Still trying desperately to achieve his quickly fleeting victory, Belial smiled his devilish grin, "Why, Michael, it's so fitting that you're here to witness my ultimate victory."

Michael stood there, undaunted by Belial's words. To each side of him stood the Chosen Ones; equally steadfast and unafraid. Michael then spread his angelic wings wide to reveal his true nature to Belial. "As you can see, I'm not the weak and scared man you once tortured. Now I guard these gates. And you shall not pass!"

Belial turned back quickly to reach for the gate, but in the blink of an eye, Michael shot forward and stood between Belial and his prize. A second later, the Chosen Ones joined to surround him.

Immediately, Belial called out for help, but was met with an empty response. Then, he watched as Lucifer strolled into view. He had Lizzy's body draped over one shoulder, while he dragged Jack's body beside him with his right hand and Holmes' body with his left. He dropped the trio on the ground at Belial's feet.

"I believe these belong to you?" Lucifer said.

Belial was at a loss for words. It was over and he knew it. Everything he had worked so hard for, snatched away from him at the last possible second.

"Looks like you're on your own, Belial," Michael said.

Belial looked around—from Michael and the Chosen Ones to Lucifer and the bodies of his Death Squad, then finally to his daughter—and resigned himself to the fact that he had been defeated. There was only one thing left to do. He refused to go back to his meaningless existence. If he ended it, then he would simply cease to exist, which, to him, was a far better alternative.

In his final desperate move, he pointed his sword at his

chest and jammed it forward, crying out as the blade pierced his flesh. But he also felt a calmness enter him for the first time since his fall.

"No!" Fierna cried out desperately. But it was too late. She fell to her knees with an empty look on her face, unable to process what had just happened. She had wanted him to pay for his betrayal, but not like this. Finally, a soft tear cascaded down her cheek. "Why, Father?" she mumbled softly.

Lucifer looked at Belial's body lying on the ground. "Well, that was unexpected," he said.

Then he looked at Michael, "I have a feeling we may see each other again sometime."

Michael replied, "I'll be looking forward to it."

Another clap of thunder signaled Lucifer's departure, and when the dust had cleared, the bodies of Belial and his three psychopath followers were gone, as was Fierna.

The Gates of Heaven swung open, beckoning Michael to enter, but he hesitated. He had something he needed to do first.

A voice echoed through Heaven that brought everyone to their knees. "Well done, Michael. It is only because of your faith and sacrifice that we have been victorious."

Michael responded meekly, "I was only doing my part, finally."

"Your effort will not be forgotten. Enter now and claim your place at my side."

When Michael stood silent, the voice responded, "The love you carry in your heart gave you the strength to succeed. Go now, and do what you must do with my blessing."

Michael rushed down to see Mary one last time.

***

Belial was scared when he opened his eyes, mainly because he shouldn't have been able to. He shouldn't be there, wherever there was? He shouldn't even exist anymore! Everyone knew that when an angel died, it ceased to be a singular being absorbed into the energy of creation. If that was the case, then why was his mind racing as he tried to grasp what was happening to him?

He had his answer a moment later when he heard Lucifer's voice. "Belial! I was afraid you wouldn't come back to me. Do you have any idea how hard it was for me to stitch you back together? If I had been a second later, I probably wouldn't have been able to."

"What did you do?" Belial whimpered.

"I did what I always do. I take the broken and tortured souls and I piece them back together. And, in exchange, they spend the rest of eternity in service to me. You are no different."

"How is that possible? I shouldn't be able to be here?"

"Oh, I had to work fast, to be sure. But, just as the last drop of your essence was disappearing, I snatched onto it and reeled you back in, particle by particle. And now look at you! Good as new...sort of."

Belial turned his head to look around and found that it was the only part of his body he could move. Iron chains tightly bound his arms and legs, attached to a series of metal rings jutting from the thick concrete wall from which he was suspended.

Lucifer walked toward Belial and approached a small cart nearby lined with surgical instruments. He picked up a long bone saw and waved it around. "In case you're wondering where we are? I claimed your little asylum as my own. It's quite a nice and morbid place, if you're into that sort of thing. Which, I am, of course."

He brought the blade close to Belial's chest. "Now, about that little ruse that you tried to play on me..."

Chapter 46

The rolling thunder and lightning flashing overhead amidst a blood-red sky was a grim reminder of the cosmic battle taking place. While most of the world was waking to the start of a brand-new day, unaware that Heaven was bleeding and dying for them, Mary knew exactly what was going on. If Heaven failed, life as they knew it would cease to exist.

She wept as she walked barefoot along the hard pavement back toward her apartment, the soles of her feet leaving behind a bloody trail of footprints that mirrored those she had left earlier as the battle had just begun. She had never felt so insignificant and lost in her life.

With each step, her strength waned, and she stumbled as she walked until her legs finally gave out. Physically and emotionally exhausted, she fell to the ground two blocks from her home. "I'm sorry, Michael," she cried. "I can't go on anymore. I don't have the strength to face this world alone."

For a long time she lay there, drowning in her emptiness, knowing that her true love was gone. She had feared as much from the first moment, when Michael had disclosed his purpose in this unholy war. He had tried to assure her that he would survive; that they would be free to live the life they dreamed of. But she knew. A tiny itch in the back of her mind told her he wouldn't be coming back.

As she lay face down on the cold pavement weeping, she suddenly felt something warm on her back. She rolled over and watched as the storm clouds vanished. Soon the sun was spreading its glowing fingers across a bright blue canvas overhead. A white dove flew down and landed at her feet, serving as a symbol that the battle was over.

Tears of joy flew into her eyes. "He did it! He won!"

Filled with a renewed strength, Mary jumped up and ran the rest of the way home, practically floating above the pavement. As she rushed into her apartment, she was rewarded with the sweet smell of lilacs carried along by a gentle breeze.

A shimmering light beckoned her to her bedroom. The broken shards of glass that had served as deadly missiles during the supernatural storm a short time ago now shimmered like a myriad of prisms as they reflected the rainbow outside her window that signaled the dawn of a new age.

On her bed, she noticed something that melted her heart instantly. She had always loved the sand dollar and its legend. Her father had bought her one during a trip to the Atlantic Ocean when she was a little girl, and from that moment on, they had a special place in her heart. She eagerly started collecting them, making them a central theme in her life. Throughout her small apartment, images, posters, plaques, and ceramics all portrayed this magical symbol, along with a variety of poems telling the legend to its readers.

There, on her pillow, lay the most perfect sand dollar she had ever seen. Next to it was her favorite poem, handwritten in elegant script on gold parchment, illustrating the beauty of this miracle:

There's a pretty little legend
That I would like to tell
Of the birth and death of Jesus
Found in this lowly shell.

If you examine closely,
You'll see that you find here
Four nail and a fifth one
Made by a Roman's spear.

On one side the Easter lily,
Its center is the star
That appeared unto the shepherds
And led them from afar.

The Christmas poinsettia,
Etched on the other side
Reminds us of his birthday,
Our happy Christmastide.

Now break the center open,
And here you will release
The five white doves awaiting
To spread Good will and peace.

This simple little symbol,
Christ left for you and me
To help us spread His Gospel
Through all eternity.

She heard his voice behind her, "Mary," and her knees

buckled as tears welled up in her eyes. When she turned around and saw Michael standing there, an image of perfection, she couldn't hold back anymore.

"Oh, Michael," she cried as she ran to him. "I'm so proud of you. You saved us all."

"I can't take all the credit, Mary. Your love gave me the strength to succeed."

She looked into his eyes. "What's next?"

He bent down and kissed her lips one last time. "Heaven is waiting for me to take my place."

"I know," Mary said sadly as she held him a little tighter, afraid to let go. Finally, she pulled away, wiping the tears from her eyes. "Go now. You've earned it."

Michael turned to leave and stopped short. "Just one more thing. Take care of our son. He going to grow up to be a very special young man."

Then he vanished.

Mary stood in shock for a second before placing her hands gently on her stomach. Maybe it was just her imagination, but she was sure she could feel a new life growing there. As Michael's departure had created a hole in her heart, the unborn child inside had helped to stitch that hole closed just a little bit. Now, she had a reason to go on.

The End.

Book Three Preview

Hellish

Book Three:

Vizibir

by
Scott Dokey

Chapter 1

Sometimes the forces of evil work in ways that are open for the entire world to see, their atrocities laid bare before God and man; individuals like Hitler and Stalin, who personified evil in its purist form. Usually, though, evil works just under the surface of our reality, spreading its icy tentacles into all that is good. At first, it feels like nothing more than a slight tickle, only mildly irritating, but before long, it becomes a maddening itch that can never be scratched. That's how it started with Jeremy.

On a warm Saturday morning in June, little Jeremy Daniels bounded out of bed and rushed to his bedroom window, smiling wide when he saw a cloudless, blue sky overhead. As fast as a six-year-old kid can dress himself, he pulled on a pair of jeans, two mis-matched socks, and a T-shirt that may, or may not have been dirty, then raced downstairs.

Minutes later, he held the carton of milk with both hands and gingerly poured it into his bowl of Cheerio's, proud of the fact that he'd only spilled a few drops onto the table, all while glancing back and forth at the picture of the hungry lion splayed out next to him. A dribble of milk ran down his chin after shoveling a couple of huge bites into his face, almost more than his mouth could hold, then he flipped the page to a giraffe with its long tongue snaking out and eating hungrily from the hand of a small boy about his age. A wistful smile spread across his lips.

Jeremy had just plunked another huge spoonful of cereal into his mouth, turning the page to show a troop of monkeys whispering secrets to each other, when his dad entered the room.

A tall and thin man, who wore a serious face most of the time, Nathan Daniels was unusually happy and upbeat as he passed behind his son on the way to the counter, where the coffee maker sat with a freshly brewed pot in its belly. After pouring himself a cup, he sat down across from Jeremy, taking a long sip before putting the cup down.

"Are you excited for today?"

Jeremy nodded. "First, I wanna see the lions, then the elephants, then the snakes, then the—"

Nathan chuckled, "Wow, slow down, kiddo. We'll have plenty of time to see everything."

Jeremy pouted for a second. "I know. It's just that, we don't get to do stuff like this very much. And I want today to be special."

Nathan looked at his son. "I know, but you have to understand how important my work is."

"More important than me?"

Nathan was silent for a moment. Then his phone rang.

Jeremy listened with the familiar uneasiness coiling up in his stomach as his dad talked in his distinct business tone to the person on the other end.

Nathan looked at Jeremy for a second before he turned and walked to the corner of the room, where he continued the conversation.

"Sorry, kiddo," Nathan said when the call was done. "I'm

afraid I have to go in to the office for a while today. Something's come up in this case I'm working on. I'll have to take a rain check on the zoo."

For a few minutes, Jeremy tried to be brave; tried to hold back the tears. If he had been older, he might have understood what the name Nathan Daniels meant among prosecuting attorney notoriety. But he was just a child, with childish hopes and childish dreams. He didn't know the world of grownups; didn't want to know; didn't deserve to know. Not at his age.

Finally, the dam burst and he ran to his room, crying like he had done so many times before.

That's when it all began.

***

A soft sound, like the flutter of tiny wings, drifted to Jeremy's ears, breaking through the sadness and jolting his curiosity. He looked up from his tear-soaked pillow and was surprised to see a soft, green point of light hovering a few inches from his face.

His first thought was that a firefly had somehow found its way into his room. Then he realized two things: first, it was morning; and second, the thing floating in front of him had no visible body. It was just a glowing orb that hung there in the air for a minute before it suddenly disappeared. But right before it did, it whispered his name.

Instantly, Jeremy forgot about his dad's broken promise and ran to his mom to tell her about the glowing light. Unfortunately, the condition he found her in was one of a drunken stupor, with an empty bottle of whisky on the end table next to the couch where she laid, the television blaring away and her cloudy eyes trying to focus on whatever show was playing. A cigarette dangled precariously in her fingers, threatening to drop a pile of ashes onto the floor. Barely able to lift her head from the arm of the couch, she looked at him in a confused way while he recreated his close encounter for her.

Her words were slurred as she spoke. "What in the hell you talking about, boy? Are you going crazy? If it's attention you're after, I'll give you attention! How 'bout I beat your ass and really give you something to think about?"

In just a few minutes, Jeremy's heart was ripped out and thrown back into the void where his father had tossed it only a short time before. He ran back to his room, which had become his harbor of refuge from this hurtful world he had been forced to live in.

As soon as he buried his head back into his tear-stained pillow, the soft buzzing drifted to his ears once more, lifting him from his saddened state and bringing a smile back to his lips. This time, the creature seemed to shine a little brighter, buzz a little louder, feel a little warmer. It darted back and forth in front of Jeremy a few times, like a crazed, happy-go-lucky insect. It flitted around, tickling the end of his nose, brushing against his cheek, and nuzzling up to his ear.

A soft voice then whispered into his ear a single word, "Vizibir."

Chapter 2

A soft knock sounded on Jeremy's bedroom door and immediately his little alien friend vanished.

His door creaked open slowly, and his dad peaked his head in. "I've got to go, kiddo. Hopefully, this will only take a few hours and I'll be home before you know it. Maybe we'd still have time to go out for ice cream, or something?"

These were hollow words that Jeremy had heard numerous times before.

"Since Janice has decided to drink her breakfast today, I've asked your Aunt Sophie to come over and watch you until I get back," Nathan continued.

Sophie stepped from the hallway. She was a young lady with short, blond hair, and bright blue eyes. She resembled a younger version of his mother, only she had a clear head and a sense of self-pride—and she was sober. A very pixie-like demeanor radiated from her.

"Hey, Jeremy," she said. "How's it going?"

"Okay, I guess," he lied.

Nathan turned to Sophie, "You have my number in case you need to reach me?"

"Yep, sure do."

She looked over at me. "Don't worry, Sweetie, we're going to have lots of fun today. I figured we'd watch a couple of movies, maybe make some popcorn, order a pizza?"

Even in his state of hopelessness, Jeremy's eyes lit up, just a little, at the mention of popcorn. The buttery smell, the salty flavor, even the popping sound echoing through the kitchen was a weakness of his. The very thought of that melted butter flowing down his throat as he crunched on a handful of the magic corn had him thinking that maybe this day would turn out all right after all.

He couldn't have been more mistaken.

After a few minutes, he heard the front door close and his dad's car backing out of the garage. As he walked out of his bedroom toward the family room, he noticed that his mom no longer occupied the couch in the living room.

A minute later, Jeremy was a little more enthusiastic, even anxious, as he sat down in front of the TV, waiting for the pizza party to start. Sophie had that way about her, making everything just a little brighter during the darkness. His stomach started to rumble a little, trying to coax the pizza delivery guy through some arcane hunger communication to get there as fast as possible.

Sophie walked over to him, carrying a couple of movies in her hands.

"Okay, kiddo, which would you prefer, 'Toy Story' or 'The Lion King'?

"Those movies are for babies!" Jeremy said. "I'm six-and-a-half now. I want something with action, like the 'Power Rangers'."

She giggled, "Six-and-a-half now, is it? When did you get so big?"

After rifling through the large collection of movies, which filled a large bookshelf in the corner of the family room, she finally pulled one out.

"If it's 'Power Rangers' you want, then it's 'Power Rangers' you'll get."

A minute later, Jeremy was watching his favorite show and thinking that this day might turn out pretty great after all. Then he realized that it was his aunt, and not his mother, that he was enjoying this moment with. Suddenly, it wasn't so fantastic anymore.

He looked at his aunt for a second, taking in her carefree, fun-loving essence, and thought that his mom was probably like that at one time. Somewhere along the road, the pressures of life, marriage, motherhood, took their toll and zapped all the joy from her spirit.

The ring of the doorbell snapped him from his moment of wistful thinking, and immediately he smelled the scent of pepperoni pizza wafting through the house.

Then he heard Sophie's voice shouting from the living room; "I said, take your hands off me, now!"

Jeremy jumped from the couch and ran toward her cry. As he rounded the hallway, he saw her struggling in the doorway, trying to escape the delivery guy's grasp. Even though he wore the uniform of one of the most important people in this world, the look in his eyes and the tone in his voice was more fitting to that of a hardened criminal.

"Listen, bitch," he said. "I want my stuff back, and I want it now!"

Sophie yelled back, "You'll get your stuff back, asshole, when I'm fucking ready to give it back, and not before!"

The not-so-nice delivery guy responded by slapping her hard across the face, sending Sophie slamming backward against the wall with a mixture of shock and rage on her face. Jeremy ran forward and kicked the man as hard as a six-and-a-half-year-old could kick.

Once again, the guy's hand swung around, this time catching Jeremy on the side of the head and sending him sprawling to the floor.

As Jeremy lay there on the floor crying, with blood seeping from a cut on the back of his ear where the man's nails had caught his skin, he heard the familiar buzzing echoing in his ear, and saw the mysterious green light fluttering before him, bigger than before. Then it shot forward and struck the attacker in the middle of the chest, sending him flying backward into the stone pillar that supported the roof covering the front porch. His body slumped to the ground, leaving a streak of blood behind to mark where his head had hit.

Somehow Janice had managed to arouse herself from her drunken stupor in response to Sophie's outcry, and peeked her head into the living room.

"Oh my god," she cried. "What in the hell happened here?"

By this time Sophie was sitting up, propped against the wall. "I'm not sure," she said. "It all happened so fast."

She turned to me. "I saw it. I saw the light, right after he hit you. It flew forward and hit him right in the chest."

His mother, in all her drunken splendor, looked at Jeremy with disgust written all over her face. "What have you done, Jeremy?"

Author Bio

Growing up in the shadow of Notre Dame's Golden Dome, Scott Dokey developed a strong affinity for the arts, learning at a young age the joy of transforming an empty page into something magical. Eventually, as an adult, his creative endeavors expanded to include writing and filmmaking. Focusing primarily on subjects with horror and supernatural aspects, he became an award-winning screenwriter, and has produced and directed three short films and a no-budget feature film.

Scott currently lives in Southern California with his wife, Jennifer, and their daughter, Kaylee, enjoying the sweltering 120° summer heat. Of course, 85° in January more than makes up for it.

To find out more about his work visit his website at www.scottdokey.com

Be sure to check out Hellish Book One: Tortured Souls